Fugitive Light

Middle East Literature in Translation

Michael Beard *and* Adnan Haydar, *Series Editors*

Fugitive Light

MOHAMED BERRADA

Translated from the Arabic by Issa J. Boullata

With a Foreword by Michael Beard

 SYRACUSE UNIVERSITY PRESS

Originally published in Arabic as *Al-Daw' al-Harib.* Copyright © 1993 by
Al-Fanak, Casablanca, Morocco.

The paper used in this publication meets the minimum requirements of
American National Standard for Information Sciences—Permanence
of Paper for Printed Library Materials, ANSI Z39.48–1984.∞™

Library of Congress Cataloging-in-Publication Data
Barādah, Muḥammad
Ḍaw' al-hārib
Fugutive light : a novel / Mohamed Berrada ; translated from the
Arabic by Issa J. Boullata with a foreword by Michael Beard.—1st ed.
p. cm.—(Middle East literature in translation)
ISBN 0-8156-0749-0
I. Boullata, Issa J., 1929– II. Title. III. Series.
PJ7816.A6538 D3913 2002
892.7'36—dc21
2002008074

Manufactured in the United States of America

For Sonallah Ibrahim
these fleeting moments,
continuously fugitive.

MOHAMED

For my brother Kamal,
Palestinian artist semper fidelis,
this translated novel
about fugitive light
he always seeks.

ISSA

What, then? Did you imagine that I would write about all this misery and all this joy, and that I would cling fast to it with my head lowered? Did you really imagine I would do that if I had not been preparing—with a hand trembling a little—the maze I would venture into, conveying to it my discourse for which I would open vaults and provide galleries, and which I would distance from itself? Only so would I epitomize its direction and disfigure it. For it would then be a maze in which I would be lost, and from which I would finally come out to meet eyes I would never be able again to look straight into.

Doubtlessly, there are many persons like me who write so that they may no longer have a face. Therefore, don't ask me who I am, and don't say that I must remain myself: for these are the ethics of the civil status that circumscribe our personal identification papers, which should otherwise leave us free when it is a matter of writing . . .

—By a writer whose name slipped
my mind (Michel Foucault??)

Mohamed Berrada was born in Fez in 1938. He graduated from the Department of Arabic Literature, Cairo University, in 1960. On his return to Morocco, he worked for the Moroccan Broadcasting Corporation and became an active member of the Socialist Union for Popular Forces, which played a key role in the achievement of Moroccan independence. Having earned a doctorate at the Sorbonne in 1973, Berrada played an important role in Moroccan letters, as a writer, a critic, and professor at Mohammad V University since 1964. He is the author of a collection of stories, *Salkh Al-Jild* (*Skinning*, 1979), as well as three novels, *Lu'bat Al-Nisyan* (*The Game of Forgetting,* 1987), *Al-Daw' Al-Harib* (*Fugitive Light,* 1993), and *Mithl Sayf lan Yatakarrar: Mahkiyyat* (*A Summer Never to Be Repeated,* 1999). He translated works by Roland Barthes, Mikhail Bakhtin, Jean-Marie Gustave Le Clézio, Abdelkebir Khatibi, and others.

Issa J. Boullata teaches at the Institute of Islamic Studies at McGill University, has published several scholarly works on Arabic literature, and translated a number of Arabic poems and books. He is author of *Trends and Issues in Contemporary Arab Thought* (1990), and editor of *Critical Perspectives on Modern Arabic Literature* (1980) and *Literary Structures of Religious Meaning in the Qur'an* (2000). His translations include Jabra Ibrahim Jabra's *The First Well* (1987), Chada Samman's *The Square Moon* (1994), Mohamed Berrada's *The Game of Forgetting* (1996), and Emily Nasrallah's *Flight Against Time* (1987, 1997).

Foreword

Michael Beard

THERE IS A SCENE in *La vita nuova* that occurs a year after Beatrice's death, where Dante, in passing, describes himself drawing a sketch of an angel. We don't usually think of Dante as an artist, but for one brief moment there it is. Robert Browning was so fascinated by that scene that he comments on it (in his poem "One Word More"):

> You and I would rather see that angel,
> Painted by the tenderness of Dante,
> Would we not?—than read a fresh Inferno.

Mohamed Berrada's *Fugitive Light (Al-Daw al-harib,* 1993) is not a painting. But this story, or parable, or fictionalized memoir of a painter, is so unlike his previous novel, *The Game of Forgetting,* that readers are likely not to recognize his style. It is as if Berrada had left the world of his previous success, veered off into another medium, and started sketching angels. *The Game of Forgetting (Lu'bat al-nisyan,* 1987; also translated by Issa J. Boullata) is famous for its psychological subtlety and post-modernist self-awareness, which has made it a popular text in courses on Middle

Eastern literature. *Fugitive Light* makes an appeal of a totally different kind.

Indeed, it may seem not just different but a kind of retraction, a 180-degree turn, a manifesto of surfaces. We find ourselves, when we read *Fugitive Light,* entering a genre that draws on a whole other set of narrative traditions, in which a painter's career is projected against the backdrop of his erotic life. It was Northrop Frye whose criticism emphasized so powerfully the generic distinctions between the novel and the romance forms: "The romancer does not attempt to create 'real people' so much as stylized figures which expand into psychological archetypes. . . . That is why the romance so often radiates a glow of subjective intensity that the novel lacks, and why a suggestion of allegory is constantly creeping in around its fringes."* In the novel we expect psychological complexity, round characters, identities with depth seen against a closely observed social background; in the romance we expect flat characters, personae defined in superlatives—what Frye called archetypes. Fatima must be eminently beautiful. Al-'Ayshuni, to balance her symmetrically, must be eminently experienced and creative. To say, for instance, that Fatima's dream in chapter one is a characteristically male fantasy rather than a dream any woman is likely to have had, in fact, is less to criticize the book than to name the genre.

A reader with a taste for romance as a separate, non-novelistic form may discriminate between kinds of romance, so that *Daphnis and Chloe, The House of Seven Gables* and Danielle Steele's *Sunset in St. Tropez* will not end up on the same shelf. *Fugitive Light*

---

* Northrop Frye, *Anatomy of Criticism* (Princeton, N.J.: Princeton Univ. Press, 1957), 304.

explores a well-known and acknowledged romance theme, the parable of the artist and model. As a source of fascination, this theme did not begin with Picasso. We find it in European literature as early as Balzac's Pierre Grassou and his Sarrazin. Poe's "Oval Portrait" is a peculiarly concentrated form of the parable. In Persian literature there is the example of the opening section of Sadeq Hedayat's *The Blind Owl* (1936). (The reader may feel on the verge of it in the dialogue scene of Thomas Mann's "Tonio Kröger.") It is such an established variation on the romance plot that in Alfonso Cuarón's 1998 film version of Dickens's *Great Expectations,* Pip was simply remolded as an artist, Estelle as his model, and we were expected to notice that this was a logical variation—from Bildungsroman to Kunstlerroman. Closer to *Fugitive Light* is the parable of Alberto Moravia's *La noia* (1960; translated into English as *The Empty Canvas*).

With its physical, secular, visual intensity and its acute awareness of outline and color, *Fugitive Light* is the sort of story for which we often use the term "Mediterranean." American readers are not used to the light on the other shore of the Mediterranean, but that is where Berrada sketches his angels.

Michael Beard
University of North Dakota
May 2002

A Note of Thanks

I WOULD LIKE TO THANK my friend, poet Abdellatif Benyahya, for the tape he provided me containing the story entitled "The Illness of Zein" by Ahmad Al-Murabit. I would also like to mention the help provided me by the character of Mademoiselle Beaunon, the protagonist of the novel entitled *Les dimanches de Mademoiselle Beaunon* by Jacques Laurent (Editions Grasset, 1982), for without her pioneering and her outstanding intelligence, Fatima Quraytis would not have been able to face her ordeal in a foreign land.

Rabat, 1988–93
M. B.

Fugitive Light

1

HE WAS RELAXED as he lay on the wide quilt inside the large veranda facing the sea and the Spanish shore visible to the naked eye on a clear day despite the distance. The muezzin's voice was still announcing the setting of that day's sun, while he was attracted to a vague idea he had read or heard about, regarding something that was born between evening dusk and the darkness of night. Where and when? His soul was always charged with obscure feelings at such an hour, with a bundle of thoughts. He began to drift and follow all that occurred to him, his mind crowded with reminiscences and scenes as it jumped from one realm to another looking for a station to rest at . . .

He stood up quickly and moved his arms in gymnastic motions. He pressed the light button. A lamp in a wicker shade was turned on and a canvas on an easel appeared, near which were tubes of paint, pencils, and a brush soaking in a half-filled glass. For several days, he had been trying to ravish the whiteness of the tight canvas. All the details were clear in his imagination but his fingers were unable to take off. At a given moment, he would think that an inner spark was sweeping his hesitation away and he would prepare himself to begin. But his hand would suddenly stop before touching the canvas, so he would return the brush to the glass and give himself up to unexpected imaginings that would impede his élan and postpone the beginning moment of painting. He picked up a newspaper from the floor and his eyes ran over the news printed in a box:

"Several homes suffer from day and night attacks by insects known as 'oil thieves,' which have multiplied in recent years because of the lack of disinfection in al-Wad al-Harr, whose sewers have often burst in the main streets of Casablanca."

He said in an audible voice, "But I saw oil thieves in my kitchen yesterday, flying with their transparent wings, although I never use oil. Were they looking for butter, then? I try not to use insecticides because I always suspect companies producing them of actually promoting the multiplication of oil thieves and other insects. Otherwise, they would have gone bankrupt a long time ago. In other words, we can deduce that their chemicals are totally ineffective."

He heard the doorbell ring, so he got up to open the door, still thinking of the details of the oil thieves problem and the possibilities of its development.

He opened his mouth but couldn't say a word. A smooth, exciting air enveloped her face. Her honey-colored eyes shone with an equivocal look and her chestnut hair was cut short à la garçonne. Her gown hung down her body, showing its graceful form at the lines of her bosom and waist.

"I believe I'm at the home of artist al-'Ayshuni. Isn't that so?"

"Indeed, indeed. Please, come in. Oh, I remember. You're Miss Fatima, who spoke with me on the telephone."

Her face was friendly, her words flowed with spontaneity and affection. She spoke about painting and literature, then moved to what she had seen on the streets. She quoted what her female friend said about her father, who snorted whenever he copulated with her mother. And she asked with nonchalance: "Is there a scientific or medical explanation for this phenomenon?"

He interrupted, "I don't think you're a journalist, as you claimed."

"What, then, do you think I am?"

"A potential painter or a writer: your enthusiasm is infectious."

She smiled, "Not exactly. I'm an admirer. But my admiration is complex. I haven't seen your paintings but I know a lot of the things you said. I've come to know them through a woman who shared everything with you and speaks with reverence and veneration about you."

The situation was more complicated than he had thought. Reverence and veneration? This meeting did not seem to be like the other meetings, which had left him with an impression of routine and sameness. He went toward the inner room as he asked her whether she would like to have a drink. She said she would take the same drink he did. Then she added, "I know that at this time of day you take gin and tonic with lots of ice." He nodded in agreement and was more puzzled. The two glasses held by the fingers gave a chink as they moved and the ice cubes touched their inner edges. He looked straight at her and noticed a collusive smile on her lips. He felt he was in an unprecedented situation. He wondered how he should act in order to uncover the identity of the intruding woman sitting next to him and speaking with spontaneity and merriment as though she were an old friend. He tried to change his tone, using expressions like "In fact" and "The reality is . . ." But the sentences stumbled in his throat and he leaned backward, crossed his legs, then raised his eyes to look at her.

She laughed, "Don't trouble yourself. I'm an admirer as I told you. I've come to spend the evening with you. Does my presence bother you? Didn't I appeal to you?"

"God forbid. Your beauty is unsurpassable."

"That's it, then. There's no need to occupy your mind with who I am. I want to converse with someone who can understand the deep vibrations of my soul in this city that hides behind words of copper. I've been in Tangier for a month and I haven't yet met a man who would talk with me without putting his finger on his fly ready to undo his zipper."

Al-'Ayshuni said, "Too bad for you." Then he added, "No. Our city is like all others, for it also has pious people and mystics. Had you met a mystic, he would have recited spiritual love poems to you or he would have made you into a phantom of light."

"I've come to you, and I know I'll find with you what I've missed elsewhere."

Their eyes met in a long, intent look. Al-'Ayshuni got up and began to pace the room slowly. He then turned to her. "But this way, you're putting me outside the game. You can't continue to be incognito, for that will impede my attempt to weave the immediacy you desire."

In moments of silence punctuating their conversation, al-'Ayshuni tried to survey the faces of the women he knew in Tangier or elsewhere, hoping to find that of the one who had, as his visitor claimed, told her everything about him. The list was long, the figures varied, and all that variety of women he knew was nothing but an image of the contradictory and conflicting moments he had lived for over fifty years. "I've known as many women as there are varieties of possible desires and whims. And there was always some justification to meet a woman outside

love, passion, and internal ecstasy . . . Was that some kind of ad-
diction? Fear of loneliness? Or was it some compensation for
things I don't know?"

He was stunned to hear her announce her name. She told
him she was the daughter of Ghaylana, his sweetheart whom he
had not seen in years. That name, in particular, had not occurred
to him as he surveyed in his mind the faces of the women he
knew. Was it because she was the nearest to his soul? Ghaylana,
the blond, round-faced woman with a full bosom and firm legs,
and with an ambitious and strong personality—could she give
birth to such a soft young woman with dreamy eyes? The last
time he saw her was when he was returning from Gibraltar on
board a ship plying between the two shores of the Mediterranean. She was wearing a yellow dress and a navy blue hat with
a wide brim, and her face was radiant with cosmetic touches and
beautifying powders. She rushed to him with her usual spontaneity and kissed him on both cheeks, asking about his health,
his condition, and his art; and she told him that she was now well
settled in Spain for purposes of work and that her situation improved after she had left her male friend who exploited her body
in Madrid . . .

It was a bright night amid his monotonous days and harping
adventures. She had promised to ask about him whenever she
came to Tangier but she disappeared and he continued to wait for
the beautiful dream to recur.

"You're therefore Ghaylana's daughter by her first husband?"

"The first and last. My father, too, has not married again. He
still lives in Fez. I left my daughter, Nada, with him after my
divorce."

"You've had time to get married and be divorced? I used to

think you were in Spain for your studies, for this is what Ghaylana used to wish."

"Studies don't prevent marriage. At any rate, there were special circumstances behind all that. Circumstances, yes, I mean circumstances. You know better than I what circumstances are."

Her smile returned to disperse the seriousness that had infiltrated into their conversation. She said she did not yet feel his merry-go-lucky personality, the defiant character that would cling to the here and now.

"You're seeking the image your mother painted of me."

True, but more than that, she sought a certain dealing with people and life. She could not accept things as they had revealed themselves to her in the last three years: dreary, harsh, intertwined with deception and self-interest. She had read a lot and her memory had stored beautiful images and words. Her mother had accustomed her to like people and her father had brought her up on his abundant kindness and taught her how to love nature, singing, and people's company. He worked a few hours only and came back home to listen to songs and to smoke dope. From time to time, he went out for fun and was surrounded by women, and there was dancing, laughter, entertainment, and rapture. Days changed, but her father didn't. He moved slowly. He scoffed at everything. He opened his home to everyone and cared for nothing but peace of mind and living within his own private perpetuity, despite his love for Ghaylana (a love he developed after marriage, not before it). He could not bear her excessive vivacity and her preoccupation with securing the future. She returned to Tangier, where she had been born, and he stayed in Fez, living his life in the same manner. By his side, Fatima acquired this ebullient, alluring temperament abounding with joie de vivre even in moments of bitterness and disappointment.

Al-'Ayshuni asked, "And does someone like you know what disappointment is?"

"Oh! What you call it is not important, but I've experienced a lot of things. My marriage was a deceptive story. I thought he loved me but I discovered I was merely a station in his life. He married me when we graduated from college, then he went away to continue his studies and sent me the divorce papers when I had a fetus in my womb . . . But all this is behind me now. My mother stood by me, having realized her mistake in leaving me blindfolded and adrift in my father's world of embroidered dreams. I knew nothing about her private life and how she got her money and was able to give gifts. She took me back after my bad experience and began to speak to me in the language she knew well, a language I didn't know. Other aspects of her life began to be revealed to me, and problems no longer frightened me. A true friendship arose between my mother, Ghaylana, and me, and doors that were formerly closed now opened before me . . . And through her conversations, I got to know you. You do have a special place in her heart. And in turn, I've become an admirer of yours because of what she related to me about you. I'm astonished at the story of both of you together, for your temperaments are far apart. Am I mistaken?"

Fatima spoke as the cold night breeze of April blew, mixed with sounds and mutterings reaching the veranda that faced the sea. Al-'Ayshuni delved into the details of that unexpected scene. Sometimes he thought he had lived through that meeting earlier or that it had appeared to him one noontime between sea and sky when his eyes were closed. He felt that his own personality had vanished and was replaced by this creature. He listened with interest and was stunned by this soft woman who had intruded upon his solitude. But he did not want to continue under the influence of this numbness. He thought of how he could recapture his image drawn by Ghaylana for her daughter. He cleared his throat, hit his knees with the palms of his hands, then stood up.

"Let's go in to the drawing room," he said. "The stinging cold is getting sharper."

He searched for familiar words to break the intense moment a little: "Welcome, welcome. What a great day it is to be honored by the presence of Lalla Fatima, dear gazelle that she is."

He turned on the television set and a Spanish announcer appeared, who was giving an investigative report on the phenomenon of illegal cohabitation of men and women in France. The announcer said that the number of persons living in such secret agreement rather than in matrimony reached two million couples and that the Church was worried about the dangerous spreading of this phenomenon. But what did those concerned say about this matter? They were optimistic and happy because living together freed the couples from the bonds of marriage and made them always conduct an open life that needed daily effort to refresh their love.

A sociologist said that that was merely a play on words because most of those couples living together without marriage contracts did so under one roof and begat children. In his opinion, their rejection of the institution of marriage was one of the effects of the 1968 student revolution. The important thing was for the state to find a legal status for the children born as a result of this free companionship, etc.

Al-'Ayshuni asked Fatima for her opinion on the subject. She responded that that arrangement could be better than marriage, especially if the couples living together did not embark on begetting children until they were sure of their feelings.

His laughter rang out. "And will such sure feelings be possible even after the passage of twenty years?"

The next item was about a demonstration organized by neo-Nazis in West Germany on the occasion of the death of Hermann Hesse, Hitler's right-hand man. Strong young men tried to break police barriers and a large procession of supporters shouted Nazi slogans. A television reporter asked one of them about his opinion of Hitler and he answered, "For me, he is a god!"

"Everything is possible," al-'Ayshuni continued. "But I can't always remain in touch with the whirlpool. I need to cut myself off from the outside world and spend long hours alone, sometimes consecutive days, listening to my bones, as they say, slowly recollecting what I've seen, heard, and read. Without those intervals, I feel I'm an empty barrel, moving automatically and hardly able to pick up what goes on around me. In such a situation, I loathe myself and seek solitude. My relatives and friends excuse me and say, 'He's an artist, ignore what he does. He lives according to his whims, and is sometimes happy and sometimes depressed.' "

Fatima listened to him with interest, but she did not comment on what she heard. She raised her glass, asking whether it was possible to have it replenished. Al-'Ayshuni said his home was all hers and she could pour out herself whatever she wished to drink, the bottles were in a wooden box near the television set. At the same moment, he pressed another button on the remote control and an announcer on the national channel appeared, who was reading the evening newscast. Fatima said she had not watched Moroccan television since her arrival in Tangier and al-'Ayshuni answered that its achievements were many, thank God, and that she did not have to worry herself about it. Tangier, he said, was set for entertainment and those who visited it took into consideration that they would lay themselves open, during their stay in it, to what was happening on the other shore of the Mediterranean. Nevertheless, there was no harm done if she watched a little of what the talents of the national channel offered. What were the male and female announcers saying?

"The honored visitor expressed his admiration for the wonderful scenes and the variety of natural resources that God had endowed us with. He said he was certain the region of al-Hasima was poised to embark on prosperity by virtue of the government's development program that the officials made known to him . . ."

"I don't think you've ever visited al-Hasima," al-'Ayshuni remarked.

"No."

"Let's then postpone visiting it until this promised prosperity has been achieved so that we may benefit from it."

". . . In the House of Representatives, this afternoon's session was devoted to the ministers' responses to oral questions posed by the honorable representatives, mostly related to the citizens' purchasing power and high prices, as well as to the situation of prisons and the condition of prisoners, the problems of migrant workers, the issue of schools for Moroccan students in Ceuta and Melila, and the sale of certain lands to private owners.

"In their responses, the ministers made it clear that applicable solutions were on their way and that they understood the criticisms of the representatives. But they added that, despite their knowledge of the problems, they were hampered by limitations, especially in the circumstances of the world's financial crisis and its reflections on the national treasury. Therefore, the representatives asking questions should take the difficult circumstances into account. The Minister of Finance noted that he did not approve of the expression 'the downslide of the dirham,' now current among people and in the press, because the dirham did not downslide but its price went up and down in accordance with objective measures imposed by international financial circles. The word 'downslide' was thus used with bad intention to cast doubt on the wisdom of our financial policy. The minister added that, from now on, we should avoid using the word 'downslide' lest we should increase the citizens' confusion. The dirham, thank God, was on a firm footing that allowed it to ascend and descend, and there was no need for anxiety. Everyone should respect the national currency and deal with it in suitable words. The representatives of the majority party applauded the Minister of Finance's explanation full of zeal and fervor . . ."

The doorbell rang with some insistence. Al-'Ayshuni exchanged a quick look with Fatima as though inquiring whether she would be inconvenienced by such a visit. She shrugged her shoulders, signalling her indifference, and continued to smile.

At the door stood al-Dahmani, with his thickset medium stature, his black shining hair, his thick eyeglasses, and his husky voice that did not allow him to reach a higher tonality.

"Are you asleep or awake, sir?" Then, noticing Fatima, he added, "I've come at an inconvenient time, haven't I, my dear al-'Ayshuni."

"No, not at all. Come in, come in. This is a friend, or rather an admirer as she presents herself. And we're sitting and watching television for entertainment."

"Such be good entertainment, or else none. For often have I heard you say, 'A beautiful woman lengthens one's life.' Isn't that so, Lalla?"

Fatima's face brightened as she stretched out her hand to him. Al-Dahmani bowed as he took it and touched it with his lips in a motion betraying his experience in this field.

Al-'Ayshuni said, "Si* al-Dahmani is a friend who encourages and sponsors artists. He has an excellent gallery in the capital and owns the largest number of paintings by Moroccan painters, dead and alive."

"I and all I own are at your service. May the Lord keep you, Lalla, and may He also keep our artist. I wonder, is there any new painting or not?"

Al-'Ayshuni pointed to the white canvas on the veranda and said that the internal urge had not happened yet and that he had spent long hours contemplating, in pursuit of questions and of phantoms of fugitive paintings. Al-Dahmani interrupted him, saying he should move his fingers instead of taxing his brain, for he was now known for his style and subjects and was in no need of change or renewal. Al-'Ayshuni did not agree with him because he was no longer content to stay his course and continue to paint in the same style. He had spent many years painting naked female models, still lifes, and scenes from Tangier neighborhoods. He no longer found pleasure in that now. It was as if personification in his paintings cut short the vivacity and the vague associa-

*In the Moroccan dialect, "Si" means "Mister."

tions that every face or human mass or group of things and movements gave rise to. He was trying to explain to al-Dahmani that transformation which urged him to search for a living pulse that would not be obliterated by lines and colors, a living pulse that instead became the starting point for creating harmonious circles and shades before the eyes. But al-Dahmani listened to him halfheartedly and gave his attention to Fatima, then asked them both to make haste to go out to dine with him in one of the restaurants.

Ending a conversation that did not interest him much, he said, "As long as I'm buying from you beforehand ten paintings in your old style, why don't you hurry up and finish them? This is my question."

After some hesitation, Fatima said, "I've understood that what concerns Si al-'Ayshuni is something else. He wants to find a suitable form for his feelings and for his relation to the world. At any rate, words in this instance can't explain anything."

Al-Dahmani said, laughing, "I would like to know: are you on my side or his?"

Al-'Ayshuni looked gratefully at Fatima and stretched out his hand toward her. She stood up and clung to him, her cheeks blushing and her honey-colored eyes lighting up.

At the restaurant, al-Dahmani behaved like a great lord in order to conceal his nouveau riche status. He ordered champagne, lit up a Cuban cigar, and began to talk about his factory's making ready-made clothes. In the past month, he had produced five thousand blouses for a German company and now orders were coming to him from Holland, France, and Belgium. His problem was with the seamstresses and the banks but, despite all the difficulties, he was able to make sizable profits. "Thank God for His gifts. Who would believe that I began with artists' paintings? Do you remember Monsieur Stéfano? He was the one who advised me to buy paintings and keep them until their value rose. And so I did. The opportunity then came, and I was at the front. One must strike while the iron is hot. The matter does not need literacy and diplomas. I saved myself a lot of trouble by marrying my two secretaries together. They are at present the ones in charge of running everything in the factory. I can now sleep with peace of mind and not be afraid they would agree behind my back with another company . . . Or does Lalla Fatima wish to be my third secretary? I have no objection to that."

After a moment of silence, al-'Ayshuni said, "I became acquainted with you when you put on my first exhibit, but I did not understand the secret of your attraction to me and your interest in my paintings. In turn, I found you were nice but I do not know much about you."

"We all have more than one personality each. You know al-Dahmani the businessman. But I also have my childhood, my moments of solitude, my melancholy, my anxiety. I am only a human being, as the song goes, Aba al-'Ayshuni. My father used to work at a construction site at Ibn Isliman. As a child, I saw him work like a donkey for more than ten hours per day. He sent me to school and advised me to have an education so that I might have a better future. I obtained the *baccalauréat* and was employed at the Agricultural Inspection Department in Rabat. After independence, everything changed. I became an observer of a feverish race to obtain diplomas, positions, and wealth. I found myself in a difficult situation: on the one hand, I did not want to continue the same path I had drawn for myself; and on the other, I did not want to be a victim of my own ideals. Now, because I had lived in poverty, securing a good future became my obsessive preoccupation. And so, I made the adventurous move from artists' paintings to the factory of ready-made clothes. In the future, I may embark on another kind of work making greater profits. I'm not lucky like you. God sent you Monsieur Joséo, who saved you from Tamara and from being preoccupied with the necessities of daily life, so that you could devote yourself to your art . . . And I like you because you embody some of the things I dreamt of: you live to search, to read, to paint—as though you have no relation to this nether world. I found that I was hitting two birds with one stone: I make profits on the sale of your paintings and I live with you moments of liberation and freedom I cannot live with others.

"I have intelligence, thank God, and I've tried to use it in straight, honest employment but it did not give me abundant profit. Now, I'm exploiting it in dishonest monkey business and earn enough to secure my own future and that of my family. Don't be deceived by my appearance, Si al-'Ayshuni. Even I have a taste for life and its pleasures. God willing, I'll build a large villa this year at al-Souessi and I'll devote a big hall on the upper floor to a salon for the reception of male and female friends like you both, and for conversations about art and literature and for listening to music . . . I'll make it like a spiritual retreat for contemplation, mutual concord, and loving friendship. Yes, indeed, mutual concord and loving friendship."

At this moment, Fatima gave a sudden laugh she could not suppress. Al-'Ayshuni and al-Dahmani turned to her, seeking an explanation.

She said, still laughing, "I remembered an expression frequently used in Egyptian TV serials: 'You make me crazy, honey; you're wonderful, honey.' "

Having guessed what she meant, al-Dahmani said, "I'm neither honey nor butter. I'm only water, my dear gazelle."

Glasses were filled and emptied, and laughs continued. Fatima enjoyed the stories and jokes, and exchanged warm looks with al-'Ayshuni, who had regained his merriment and began to tease al-Dahmani and crack jokes with him. She began to feel that a light, rosy atmosphere was spreading its transparency and moving the inner depths of everyone and that the self of each was sinking into the region of illusions. It did not matter how that happened, nor did it matter to define the source of that ecstasy and departure to the world of bright caprice . . . That evening's party, unlike others she had been to in this city, seemed to be open to surprises, to promises of joy that thrilled one's body and dilated its pores.

In al-'Ayshuni's bed, her body shook with power and freedom as though it had regained its pulses that had been lying idle for months. She planted her fingers in his back, urging him to plunge deeper into her warm lake . . . Obscure specters loomed to her like swaying figures in the festival of desire, dominated by the bright face of her mother rejoicing at what she was seeing.

She found herself amid dozens of men and women in evening attire, exactly as she had seen in movies, all holding glasses and chattering aloud and ceaselessly laughing and smiling. She too wore a white long gown with bare shoulders and back. She looked in one of the large mirrors covering the walls of the interconnected halls and found that her hair was longer than usual. Around her neck was an old silver necklace with beads of exciting, phosphorescent frankincense and her surprisingly higher stature gave her the air of a lady of society. Men's eyes smiled and followed her, as she looked into the faces and turned around searching for al-'Ayshuni. She no longer remembered whether she had come in his company or whether he had said he would wait for her at the entrance of this large villa overlooking the sea at Cape Spartel. She took a few steps and turned around, somewhat embarrassed at the whispers of the guests and their melodious laughs and comments that, despite their sauciness, remained within the limits of the acceptable and sometimes refreshed her soul. She wondered, "Is al-'Ayshuni lost? Where am I? I don't know these faces." Nonetheless, the new situation stirred up her senses and tickled her femininity. She was at a loss how to respond to the bows of some of the guests and was annoyed at older women whose looks betrayed harshness and hatred. She continued her search, passing through the crowd, and sometimes noticed a face sideways resembling al-'Ayshuni's profile; she would get ready to attract his attention, then find out it was not he. The halls led to one another as though in circular interconnection. Her feet were tired, so she stopped at a large veranda and looked out to the garden. Behind the trees, the sea was present and yet absent, for its sound did not reach her ears besieged by the guests' mutterings and laughs. She noticed a flight of stairs on each side of the veranda, so she descended to the garden. She walked and noted that the place was spacious and that the surface of the sea seemed so wide and smooth one could walk on it. She began to lose her joy because she did not find al-'Ayshuni and did not know those people. He had promised to dance with her and to introduce her to some of his famous friends, who were not like al-Dahmani. "All doors are open before us artists," he had boasted with sarcasm. "Wealthy people need us either to decorate their villas with our paintings or to enjoy our words and our impudence. We're like salt in the food. And entertainment is a rare currency in this country, so the rich and those in high positions like to remain protected and dare not reveal their banal private lives. Do you understand why there is a demand for us? They spend years to gather a fortune through all means, then wake up to the fact that there is something they lack, so they bring the artists to adorn their meetings and evening parties. In turn, we find something in these relations that reduces our suffocation and takes us out of our state of neglect and distress. This is the name of the game, Fatima, and it is trifling and mean. In spite of that, I claim to myself that I can make something out of it that transcends my miserable circumstances, something fresh like your face and smile, from which I can give life to what appears to be calcified, violent, and redolent of deception and of beastliness clothed in rituals of artificial manners and traditional conventions . . ." When she listened to his philosophical notions, she did not find in him those mercurial and vibrant features that had been deposited in her memory through what her mother used to tell her about al-ʿAyshuni, who was ready to commit all manner of follies and who was searching for whatever dissipated distress and boredom. She was overjoyed when he informed her about this evening's party and gave her two hundred dirhams, saying, "I want you to shine tonight." She walked slowly in the paths of the garden, focusing on the shrubbery and the corners as though al-ʿAyshuni were playing hide-and-seek with her. She walked, having gradually lost her former feeling of estrangement after leaving the lit halls and the crowds of guests. Suddenly she heard the rustle of footsteps behind her, so she quickly turned around, frightened, only to see al-'Ayshuni laughing as he cleared his way through the luxuriant branches.

"I was sure you'd find me," he began.

"Where have you been hiding?" she asked, affecting anger.

"Simple story. I've just finished preparing this evening's prank. You can't imagine what I was busy doing a moment ago. It's a wonderful secret, but I'll reveal it to you because I need your help. I arrived before all the other guests and I sneaked into the villa's cellar and storage rooms, where I then planted hundreds of insects known as 'oil thieves,' a special kind imported from Australia that multiplies a thousandfold every minute. I'd like to take advantage of the presence of highly placed people here, at the party of the Secretary of State, to let them palpably suffer the power of this insect that disturbs us and makes us run after it for a long time before crushing it underfoot. They don't know it, although they trade in its name and delight our ears with television advertisements about the oil thieves and their dangers, concealing their true names with allusions and images to promote the sale of tons of insecticides. It is not fair that they should sell these insecticides without enjoying the sport of running after the insects, against which neither the green Bicon is effective nor the blue Flittox . . ."

Al-'Ayshuni spoke with animation and fire while Fatima understood nothing of what he was saying, because she did not see any connection between his words and the atmosphere of the grand evening party they were attending.

"What are you required to do?" he continued. "Something suiting your talent and beauty, an act that will bring out your charm and make the guests of the Secretary of State pant after you. Listen, my beautiful lady. I've promised the villa's owner that

I will present an interesting number that will break the monotony of the party and give the guests the excitement they lack. For the success of this number, I ask you to obey every command I give you, absolutely and without discussion. Understood?" Coming nearer to her, he placed his fingers on her forehead and temple, touching her cheeks and lips. She felt as though she were dreaming within a dream, stunned and drugged. With her eyes on al-'Ayshuni holding her hand, she followed him to the flight of stairs leading into the brightly lit hall. He spoke nonstop and she picked up only a few words of his continuous outpour uttered at record speed.

"Ladies and gentlemen," he said. "I am pleased and honored to present to you now Miss Buraq al-Hait."

A wave of muttering spread out and voices were heard asking for clarification.

Al-'Ayshuni continued in a loud voice, "The person who manages to ride Miss Buraq al-Hait will be safe from the insects known as 'oil thieves.' "

A chorus of men's voices rose from the middle of the hall, "We'll ride her, we'll ride her. What's the way to reach her protection?"

"Good question," continued al-'Ayshuni. "Miss Buraq al-Hait will begin to take off her clothes before she rises a little into the air. I beg you to control your nerves, for every forthcoming thing is at hand. Self-control is absolutely necessary so that the game may be satisfactory for all. I say: she'll take off her clothes to the tunes of classical music, so that we may be above the vulgar striptease. She will then soar above our heads and we have to run behind her. When we enter the storage rooms of the villa, she will put us to a test. The one who passes the test will have the reward of riding Buraq. Do you all agree?"

The applause expressed the guests' eagerness to see beautiful Fatima undressing. For a moment, she remained paralyzed in her place, while al-'Ayshuni fixed her with commanding eyes and she stared at his face as if she had forgotten what he had told her. He raised his hand, gesturing to the orchestra to begin playing. He smiled to encourage her to begin undressing. She moved a few steps in rhythm with the music, which started slow and gradually picked up speed. She twisted and turned, her eyes fixed on al-'Ayshuni's face as he smiled with visible joy. Fatima took the lower edge of her gown and raised it a little, revealing her crystalline, well-proportioned legs. Comments of approval rose to her ears and her cheeks blushed increasingly. She looked at no one but al-'Ayshuni: for him, for his sake alone she was stripping because he had promised to immortalize her charm in a painting. The gown rose and she rose with it, as though the hall were empty except for her and al-'Ayshuni and except for that tune that had penetrated under her skin, she knew not how, causing an inexplicable eruption in her body and planting in it a frenzied vehemence that made her unable to distinguish between things and humans.

She finally stood stark naked as on the day the midwife's hands received her when she came into this world. Music and all sounds ceased, and an unexpected silence reigned. Al-'Ayshuni's eyes scanned the voracious, ravenous faces for the effect of her charming body. He began to applaud and others followed; then suppressed shouts of admiration burst out and he beckoned to Fatima to continue what she had begun to do.

With elegance and airiness, she raised her arms upward and breathed in the fresh, cool air of the night, filling her lungs, and her body began to leave the ground. She started moving her arms and legs as though she were swimming in the air toward the veranda and hence to the main storage room of the villa. The men followed her, while the women remained behind expressing their resentment of this vulgar game. The Secretary of State mumbled an excuse to them but could not resist the joy of seeing the men having bitten the bait and run like children after the promised pleasure.

At the wide entrance of the storage room, they were surprised to see dense heaps of oil thieves, piled up and covering the floor up to their own heights. The insects effervesced and hopped with their dark red wings and long broad bodies. An extremely high pile of insects separated the men from Fatima's naked body resting at the far end of the storage room, laughing and saying in an enticing, goading voice:

"We've chosen these beautiful insects to test your daring despite their dirtiness. In classical Arabic, they're called *banat wardan* (daughters of cockroaches) in the feminine, while common colloquial usage considers them masculine; however, their femininity is concealed in their transparent wings. The dirty, equivocal, beautiful femininity now defies your virility, so don't be afraid of the horns of *banat wardan*. I'm here waiting for him who will defeat the oil thieves so that he may look down upon the universe from the height of Buraq al-Hait. Come on, then, come on."

Having arrived at this point in her dream, al-'Ayshuni asked her, "What happened then?"

"I don't remember," she answered. "I only remember your

harsh eyes and commanding looks ordering me to undress, and I could not disobey as tears welled up in my eyes. In spite of that, I smiled and began to do what you ordered."

She fell silent for a moment, then added, "You were attractive in your meanness. I didn't expect that you would transform me into a body common for all in order to amuse your friend's guests. I found out that you suddenly took a mean appearance but were, at the same time, exciting and attractive. I don't know how to express that feeling I had in the dream."

Al-'Ayshuni laughed boisterously and said, "A good omen . . . All that you've seen in the dream is good. You've discovered my personality in all its details, even the hidden aspects of it that your mother has not told you about. When I'm awake, I lose those features of my personality or rather those impulses that could make me a mean and aggressive person, who would pounce on things and on situations and live them up before philosophizing. I am not interested in knowing the cause of the transformation that has befallen me. But I beg you to stop splitting my head by repeating I'm no longer myself. Do I pester you with questions about who you are, about your real personality and your artificial personality?"

She said calmly, "I don't really understand your sensitivity about this subject."

"It's difficult for you to understand. Between you and me lie time and other things."

They were lying in bed as the day was dawning and the sun of a slow spring was getting warmer. More than one week had passed since Fatima's visit turned into a stay, and conversation between them had hardly stopped. Al-'Ayshuni was happy with this intruder who changed the rhythm of his life, despite the fact that he was not very pleased with that aspect of her personality that knew how to achieve its goal with determination and self-assurance. The white canvas was no longer neutral, for whenever he looked at it he felt it blazing under his looks with lines, curves, shades of color, and specters of a vision dancing above it: "The Inspiring Fatima." He would smile but then he would remember an expression he had read in which a writer or artist said that we wrote or painted only in moments of solitude and weakness, and that when we embraced the illusion of joy and happiness we preferred to live it first. Nevertheless, this joy that Fatima had brought did move his formerly stagnant and submissive soul bent on ruminating melancholic contemplations and seeing things in cold neutrality. With her around, everything stretched and multiplied; hidden desire began to be refreshed, to dig up the dead crust, in order to plant in him the eagerness of passion, and the pleasure of creativity and of self-realization in the outside world. Everything vanished in his mind: age, experience, disappointments, the boredom of repetition, the nihilism of déjà vu. Like the claws of a tame, soft cat that would scratch our feet as we are enveloped in sleep, the avid desire for life was awakened in al--'Ayshuni's depths by the rhythm of Fatima's presence beside him and by her tickling of his body and dreams. But what was it that he awakened in her? He did not ask; he felt he did not dare ask.

He was now strongly drawn to this desire, slowly bursting out within him like a seed, like a seminal drop arising between his backbone and his ribs and flowing deeply within him like dribbling drops of sweat dripping down his spine, one by one, till they joined together in an imaginary flowing line along his back to announce the restoration of health after hellish fever or bodily collapse. He looked at Fatima lying next to him and continued to gather the fragments of this desire as they collected in growing infatuation, restless impetuosity, and a feeling of inner fullness. He looked at her and got lost. He remembered the times when he used to ride the indomitable filly of desire leading him across wild lands and valley paths to build cities, while suppressed satanic forces deep within him exploded; he built cities populated with all kinds of creatures: jinn and humans, animals and bugs, insects and plants—all listening and obeying—in addition to snakes of rich colors, spots, and forms. Oh! Why was he always attracted to snakes and associating their twisting with the awakening of desire in his body and his imagination? A desire that built cities, amid ruins, in the manner of those cities portrayed in the stories of *One Thousand and One Nights*: panelled with ebony, marble, mosaics, and arabesques, and lined with yearnings fired up by the smells of spices and by baths storing pleasures that would come alive in the dark. Cities in which men neighed in laughable, commanding voices, the secret rhythm of whose passion was controlled by beautiful women with sweet speech and keen intelligence. He wondered what to call those days and extended hours he spent without a taste for life, when desire would be absent and would be buried under piled-up troubles and inner idleness.

He wondered about that because he did not remember, by contrast, what he had read in Dostoyevsky about eternal harmony, which was neither earthly nor heavenly, but which man was unable to bear because of his earthly character and found himself obliged, on that account, to be transformed physically or die.

How often do we die in this world?

Perhaps it is such moments that have given birth to the common saying, "I'll give my life for a few seconds, for a moment."

Such moments are neither earthly nor heavenly: What are they made of? Who dares give them a name without killing them?

His mind has often been distracted as he followed tempting illusions about the possibility of preserving those moments, of providing circumstances for them, and of issuing an announcement crowning them as "Public Property" to be sanctified and maintained, to be used by anyone who can rise to their orbit to embrace them and be enlightened by them in his worldly journey and when crossing the narrow isthmus to the next world. How much effort do we need? Can we bear to run daily after those moments? That's not the question, he said. What, then, is the question?

When his friend gets drunk and when sorrow clarifies his heart, he begins to tell his favorite story about the very beautiful young girl resembling the breeze in gentility, the moon in fullness, the gazelle in elegance, and the nightingale in sweetness of song . . . But she was afflicted with "the disease of beauty."

"As I told you," he would say, "this disease does really exist. It is well known and you may ask the inhabitants of the Dradib neighborhood in Tangier about it, for the heroine of the story used to live there. Let me summarize it for you: I was sixteen years old and used to be a boxer. After my exercises, I used to go to my aunt's where I used to see a girl whose beauty, to tell you the truth, I've never seen the like of. This girl had a disease I call 'the disease of beauty.' She liked to stay in front of the mirror for hours and hours. One day, my aunt asked me, 'What do you think of getting married?' I answered, 'To this girl, I'd love to.' She then said to me, 'It's a pity. She's a little sick, for she likes to spend most of her time in front of the mirror.' After an absence of one month from my aunt, I visited her again and asked her about the girl. She

said, 'The poor girl died.' I asked, 'What happened to her?' She
said, 'She went to the mirror and began to change her clothes and
comb her hair and look disdainfully at herself. She was not satisfied with the beauty that God had given her. So she went up to
the roof and threw herself off.' That ugly disease has no remedy,
may God protect us and all the Muslims from it . . ."

·   When his friend finishes narrating his story, al-'Ayshuni re-
peats his ardent comments on the moments of harmony and the
fragility of the human being: "That beautiful woman in your
story did not read Dostoyevsky, I am sure of that. Otherwise, she
would have become aware of the need to be transformed physically instead of dying and following a call coming to her from the
realm of the invisible. I understand why she committed suicide,
for the moments of harmony in her case were violent and sweeping, and she had nothing to help her face fatal fragility . . . The
call from the Absolute is destructive too, just as wallowing in ignominy and moral decay is. You laugh at what I'm saying to you
now because you think that what afflicted her was a mere disease,
for which you or other people invented the name 'the disease of
beauty.' But I don't agree. Never will I agree. Do you say that I
make a mountain of a molehill? So be it. I'm ready to swear to
you by all you hold to be holy and dear that I, whom you now see
sitting in front of you as a collected and cheerful being and everything, go on living only because I fill my head with ideas, illusions, and imaginings that help me bear ignominy and terror and
ward off from me the sweetness of suicide. But this is not the
question. Is there a question in the first place?

"Look at the surface of the sea water stretching across the
Strait [of Gibraltar], look at those hills distributed over the neighborhoods of Tangier, look at the people, the trees, the restaurants,

the bars, the mosques and minarets, the clusters of young men as colorful as mosaics, the throngs of tourists with full faces and with a cheerfulness stupidly settled on their shiny clean features as though they're just coming out of washing machines, look at all that your eyes can meet, and ask: How can we exist in depth inside all of that? How can we live and assimilate every moment and every event, how can we melt in all that our senses perceive and our minds imagine?"

They were lying down in bed after Fatima had finished telling her dream. Al-'Ayshuni was lost in a maze of remembrances, and associations poured down on his mind in droves according to their own logic. There was a long silence. He then jumped to his feet and began pacing to and fro before Fatima, who was surprised at his sudden enthusiasm. He gestured with his hands and fingers as his words gushed forth in an outpour of elaboration:

"What you've just related about your dream is strange and wonderful, and you can't imagine the extent of the excitement I feel at this moment. I mean that the white canvas was being filled and emptied at once through what I was imagining as I listened to you. It is as though I've found my way to what I was looking for. That movement I was listening to, that movement we bestow upon things and people which makes them look other than what they really are, as if they were a point that would not be complete until it embraced other points in a continuous chain, thus creating circles and circles, interpenetrating, adjacent, intercrossing before finally having their independent meaning and their own signs and existence . . . Perhaps the details are more important but the conception of the whole is what gives us the conviction of the importance of the particulars and the possibility of their

existence that dispenses with everything else. I feel I'm excited
and tense as I talk about something nobody sees but myself. I'll
clarify to you what has taken possession of me within. A friend of
mine who is a painter continued for a long time to paint empty
figures in the shape of robes that stood up without human bodies,
the three-dimensional perspective with cylindrical lines suggesting puffiness and nonexistence (body without soul, as we say).
For a long time, I continued to read those paintings through what
they suggested; then I began to look at them contented with
what they were. I always felt, however, that there were other
forms that could be added to those empty robes moving according to their own dynamics . . . Now, as I was listening to you
telling about your dream, it seemed to me that the vision pursuing me began to be clear after having been cloudy and hidden behind curtains of heaped imaginings. The people crowding at the
portal of my imagination wear various fashions, clashing with
one another in colors, shapes, and details. The robes, the frocks,
the modern suits, the felt overcoats, the ample pants, the flowing
shirts, the jeans, the jogging suits, and especially the dark blue
smoking attire—I don't see them in any specific order, but I see
the faces of those wearing them, moving or always ready to move.
This is what preoccupies me: How can I make those faces/fash-
ions/dispersions exist in motion? The scene is vast and expansive,
the movement in it does not cease, and I always associate these
persons in my imagination with energy and preparedness to run
after some goal, some obscure goal that is absent for those looking at them from the outside but present, no doubt, in the minds
of those ready to run. I even imagine that the scene is completed
in stages: there is an unseen person who gives the signal to the
pressing masses of packed bodies in suits and varied garments to

set out on a race; no one knows how long it is and what the hurdles in it are that the racers will encounter. The running begins, then stops. They breathe. They make circular movements with their arms. They inhale. They exhale. They rest. They wait. Then they assume again the position of readiness before dashing out. I feel that one painting is not sufficient. I am thinking of successive paintings, one following the other, or of moving pictures or of a film taken by camera. My senses and emotions are in suspense and that's why I relate what comes to my imagination, with your strange dream as my starting point. But I'm in need of an expressive section of it in which I'll be firmly lodged and which acquires its value from its own visual elements that epitomize the other means of communication . . . What stands most in my imagination is the crowd in smoking attire which I'll paint wearing various fashions: the same features and persons in white robes and red fezzes overlain with fabric of the transparency of the wings of *banat wardan;* and them again wearing dark-colored modern suits and always in a state of listening or applauding. In another painting, I'll present them in short pants revealing parts of their thighs and hairy legs, their big bellies showing and their short shirts sticking to their bodies that have a variety of shapes and lines . . . Or I'll paint them wearing golf clothing and holding golf clubs and moving their heads in friendly conversation after each strike. I know that such a style of painting will lead me to a kind of abstraction, because the crowd will dominate at the expense of individual persons and features, and because administrative ladders, ranks, and titles will disappear as well as all classification. But this is a secondary matter, I think. Do you understand what I would like to achieve? Its seed is in your dream and I'm stealing the idea from you and making the expression, the form, and the suggestions depend on painting the human 'mass,' which epitomizes the vision, I think. It is a mass that suggests movement although, within the variety of fashions and positions, it is drawn to a voice or expecting a signal, and is yet happy to obey and re-place movement by motion in the same place ("In your place, march!"). I may paint twenty or thirty paintings. From one paint-ing to the next, lines and colors will gradually change from the clear to the vague and ill-defined, from persons with different heights to figures sunken in obesity . . ."

Al-'Ayshuni stopped pacing and talking, and looked fixedly at Fatima, who had taken off all her clothes without his noticing. She stretched out her arms to him in a loud call without words. Her eyes shone with a peculiar light as the smooth morning brightness shed a veil of dreamy colors on her youthful, ebullient body. It was as though he were seeing her as she had portrayed herself in the crimson ballroom of the villa crowded with guests and flooded with chandelier lights and the radiance of joy and exultation.

His tongue lost its power to speak after he had thought he could talk for hours and hours about his paintings that were being born in the nebula of his soul, now on fire after former ex-tinction. His feet moved toward her, his arms stretching out like a bridge to the kingdom of the charming woman who, even when he was talking about other things, was sweeping all his being, penetrating his pores, and breaking all barriers and inhibitions. She took off his pajamas as he sank into a state of loss, looking into her eyes abounding with the tenderness and lust that his imagination used to weave for him in moments of solitude and boredom. Her lips began to travel with warm rhythm across his forehead, his temples, his cheeks, his neck, and his chest. They roamed about all the regions of his body while her hands helped to break the siege besetting his carnal appetite hiding behind concerns of thought, creativity, understanding the world and the others, and behind dark misgivings and anxieties that pounced on him whenever he wondered about the logic of things and of human relations around him. His lips in turn moved and his fingers picked up the electricity of the two bodies. Their obscure vibrations mumbled sounds that were unclear yet eloquent beyond the completeness of formulation and articulation. Fatima was creating her inimitable painting now: in her frenzied movements, she propped up his back against the bed's headpiece and thrust her legs around his trunk as his thighs opened up to contain her. The mumblings became clear, then vanished: "Mine . . . give me mine . . . My dear . . . mine . . . All my dear is mine . . . I . . . Oh . . . You? . . . Yours . . . [. . .]ours."

To someone watching from the veranda overlooking the sea, to some visitor coming, say, from the water kingdom deep in the Atlantic Ocean, the delirious mumbling, the clouded eyes, the harmonious movements, and the intertwined bodies would make the couple appear to be in a moment of prayer, separated as they were from time and place, and travelling toward climes whose light never dimmed, never set.

2

My God, lovers are not at fault.
It is You who put them to the test
By creating many a pretty face
Therewith captivating onlookers' hearts.
And yet You command us to overlook them
As if You created no eyes for us.
                              —*By an ancient/modern poet*

PERHAPS YOU FIND IT STRANGE that I spend long hours here on the veranda facing the sea without getting bored or tired. You go out to the city and return to find me still in the same position. That's because, at intervals, when ideas and dreams take hold of me, I run after them before transforming them into shapes that move my pen and my brush. Approximately one month before your visit, I was deep in thought, trying to remember the features of Tangier in the 1920s, during my early childhood, when the city was in its international period. I don't think you understand that period's flavor, which besets me and stirs me to run after its shadows. Since the time you went out this morning, I have been gathering the dispersed elements, scenes, words, and features of persons and of pulled-down places, in order to capture the secret of pleasure and pain. Your question about my relationship with your mother may have been what awakened my storage of dormant memories. But I feel I am less spontaneous as I talk to you, because I want to remember with you a part of my bygone past. I feel you are obscure and unfettered; I mean, you are ambiguous to me despite the clarity of your smile and the brilliance of your eyes. I feel exactly as when I sometimes stand frozen in front of the canvas, holding my brush and trying to capture the fugitive light I had felt to be present and visible in what I was painting. Excuse the tone of my speech, but it is with you alone that I can speak about what I imagine to be exactly my feeling. Now that you inform me that you will leave my home and perhaps also the city, and ask me to tell you about my relationship with your mother, I find myself troubled, perplexed, at a loss . . . That's something not natural after the experiences we lived together and the familiarity that has grown between us.

Since morning, I've been turning your question in my head and failing to extract your mother's face from the folds of spaces and the features of other people. They all pour down upon my imagination and don't leave me any room for dissecting the moments. I therefore appeal to your patience so that I may be able to dig up what is hidden and what your presence has awakened.

I am not saying that Ghaylana was just a face among the others, a woman among many I have known. Collusion between her and me bestowed upon our relationship a character of impetuosity, confrontation, and defiance. And so I became to her as she became to me the beloved-hated mirror, the mirror that conceals nothing, the mirror that we aspire to break but always yearn for tenderly. Perhaps you know nothing about the childhood of the artist who sits in front of you and I cannot relate it to you in all its details.

. . .

I was not born in Tangier. I rather came to it with my mother
when I was seven years old, after my father had suddenly died at
Dwar Lakhrab, where we lived, in the proximity of Tangier. My
mother was strong-bodied, solid by nature, and she found rest
only in work. She used to take me with her to Suq Barra [the
Outer Market], seating me beside her as she busied herself with
the sale of cheese, eggs, honey, and olive oil. She always wore the
colorful *traza* sombrero on her head, summer and winter, and she
never tired of giving buyers a good deal and demonstrating the
good quality of her merchandise. I used to have pleasure in the
souk's commotion and in playing with other children, brought to
the market by their mothers. One day, a Spanish man took my
hand and began to talk to me kindly. When my mother noticed
him, she asked him what he wanted, so he explained to her in
broken Arabic that he wanted to take me to school . . . They
talked for a long time—and I think he lured her with financial
help—so she accepted that we go with him to his home, from
which I saw the sea for the first time, I mean this house in which
we now sit. My mother felt assured and found Joséo kind and
amusing with his conversation and stories. He offered her a place
to live in at his home and promised he would take charge of my
education to make me a great painter like him. Look at the painting hanging on the right-hand wall; it's a portrait of him I painted
a year before his death. I've always been excited by that sparkle in
the midst of his dark features, as though he had a hidden sorrow
that bore down on his appearance, but the sudden sparkle suggested he had a capability for wonder and for the discovery of
what surrounded him.

Joséo is my real father. He showered me with tenderness and

accompanied me as I discovered my new world and took my first steps at school. I learned Spanish first, then he insisted that I learn Arabic with a private tutor. And in this room, I began to scrawl sketches, mix colors, and imitate his paintings. My mother was very happy because she found someone to take care of me. But she immersed herself in her "commerce" and preferred to live with one of her female friends in a room in a house near Bab al-Fahs. In a few years, she became well known in Suq Barra and clients sought her out to buy her good merchandise. On my part, I loved Joséo because he taught me many things without preventing me from having my own life experiences.

He used to talk to me about Spain and about Tangier at the beginning of this century when he first arrived as a tourist and was attracted by its light in the daytime as well as by the simple life of its people. He always reminisced, as he talked, about the stages of building Boulevard Pasteur. You do remember that street, for it still is the hub of the city. Imagine, its first name was Dar al-Salaf Street and the first edifice built on it was Dar al-Salaf al-Maghribi [Moroccan House of Loans], responsible for the payment of Moroccan debts to foreign states and the management of import benefits.

Joséo was fond of speaking about the beginnings of modern Tangier and about the ethnic groups living together in it. That must have been a response to a favorite dream of his, for he liked to meet people and speak about art, literature, and music and to frequent the Cervantes Theater and the Paris Grand Café. When we roamed about town in the evening, he used to stop at Sur al-Maʻkazin (the Retaining Wall) as we call it nowadays. He used to explain to me how that was the first wall ever built on the hill that would later embrace Boulevard Pasteur. It was a wall that held back the sand and at which travelers and those coming from Suq al-Dakhil [the Inner Market] stopped to look at the sea and take refuge from the winds.

He did not answer my question when I asked him why he refrained from marriage. But he used to show me pictures of himself in the company of elegant women and vivacious men, many pictures of romantic outings at the pavilions on Boulevard Pasteur and the other streets near the sea. It was a golden era, as he called it, because everything seemed new and people enjoyed life, and beauty was abundantly present and pertaining to all nationalities.

He used to say to me, "In Tangier I was obsessed by the illusion of discovering things as they were at point zero. I was overwhelmed by enthusiasm because I lived in a city in which the landmarks of civilization were being built stone by stone and house by house, and on the basis of a human mosaic of intermarriage, dialogue, and happy living under one sky. I forgot what I had known in my country and I was enveloped by a joy similar to my first joy when I discovered the world during my adolescence in Spain, for I found that Tangier—before Morocco's other cities—imported women's nylon stockings, Parker fountain pens, Swiss watches, radios, and refrigerators, and I was elated by the experience and its novelty and I followed it up with vigor. I frequently attended plays and recitals of classical music, and I amused myself in the carnivals organized by the foreign communities every year. Journalism flourished in all languages as though the European elite had succeeded in realizing their unity here in the territory of Tangier and in shining the lights of their civilization on this city open on two seas, joining two continents: nine

European states lived here in accordance with an international law that preserved the rights of their citizens who took pleasure in the sunshine, in prosperity, and in joie de vivre . . ."

I used to be astonished at how Joséo's heart could contain so much love for all the people and how he was careful to embrace beautiful things. During the Second World War, he was taken over by anxiety and no longer painted as he used to. I asked him about the cause of his sorrow and he said Spain was planning to occupy Tangier and join it to the protectorate regime applied in the north of Morocco. For me, it was a different thing, because adolescence made me find an opportunity for liberty in the climate of the war. I used to frequent foreign women's brothels and was particularly attracted to the beautiful Polish women who had come to Tangier after Hitler occupied their country. They used to sit in front of wooden huts in their transparent underclothes, their faces heavily painted with bright colors. I discovered the female body for the first time with a Polish woman who looked like a tender, fragile doll and knew only a few Spanish words. She often resorted to sign language, especially when complaining of crude customers as she pointed to their bite marks on her neck and nipples.

Joséo noticed my craving to visit the Polish women, so he used to tell me gently all about sex, women, and love; but I was in the grip of instinct and transitory adventures.

In 1945, Tangier regained its international status and so nightlife was revived, groups of foreigners returned, and the city assumed its former character as a den for pleasures, deals, meetings of spies, and adventures of love and sex. I remember one summer morning I was strolling near the Minzah Hotel when I saw two Italian young women. I did not hesitate to pursue them.

They asked about my age and I said I was sixteen years old. They laughed and said, "You're still at the beginning of youth. There's no harm if you waited a little before pursuing women." I said spontaneously, "I've found in you a model of the human body as I would like to paint it. I'm a beginning artist and your beauty will inspire me. I beg you to accept my request." So they gave me an appointment to come with my equipment to paint them. When we met at the hotel, they asked me what I thought was a suitable place for me to do what I requested. I said that their room was the most suitable place to paint their naked bodies. I don't need tell you the details, but that experience made me discover sex and its pleasures outside the context of the brothel and of pleasure whose price was prepaid. A week later, the time of their departure came and my eyes welled up with tears. I was overwhelmed by a sweeping sadness but the two Italian women patted me on the head and said, laughing, "Don't worry. We're confident you'll make your way successfully with women. As for painting, you've not shown us anything of it!"

My involvement in love adventures became stronger. I was fascinated by discovering women and immersing myself in painting. I enclosed myself in this bright-colored shell and hardly looked outside it. I did not even follow up the transformation happening in Tangier after the king's visit to it in 1947 except through some references of Joséo, who used to convey to me echoes of the nationalist movement. Our conversations were about art and women, about freedom, beauty, and the pleasure of identifying with nature. When I told him I was going to stop going to school, he did not object. He suggested I should make a trip to Spain to visit museums and art exhibits and to get to know Andalusia and its landmarks.

My life, however, took another rhythm because I began to face the world as though I were making my own life in the way I wished. Joséo intervened only surreptitiously, careful not to make me feel any coercion. Meanwhile, I was crazy about painting and reading, madly infatuated with women and their bodies, strongly drawn to Spain and all the pleasures it promised. I can't explain that specific direction which my life took at that time while I was at the threshold of youth. I may say without being too precise that it must have been the innate physical forces obeying primitive nature and instincts where there were no controls. Such forces impress our behavior with excessive sensibility and strengthen in us the illusion of being able to control the direction of our life. I don't exactly know how, but I'm telling you about my own situation at that time so that you may understand what I was when I came to know Ghaylana, your mother.

I was associated with a group of Moroccan, Spanish, and Italian people and we used to go out together to restaurants and dance halls and hang around in the bars of Tangier. We imitated what we heard about "the crazy years" that some young people in certain European countries went through in the 1930s. All desires and whims seemed realizable and the blood rushing in our veins blinded us to all that surrounded us. One day, my friend al-Zulali told me about a Moroccan young woman who lived in his neighborhood; he said she would accept the role of model and would sit for me to paint her naked as I had done earlier with a Spanish young woman. I was astonished at first because, having observed the behavior of Moroccan women, I was under the impression they were staid. I therefore avoided having any adventure with them. But al-Zulali told me interesting and exciting things about Ghaylana's personality and beauty that aroused my curiosity. When he introduced her to me in one of the cafés, I found her attractive. Her looks had a certain provocation, her blondness was mixed with a light reddish color, her round face had arresting delicate features, and her movements were audacious with a spontaneous coyness about them . . . Or this is how I preserved her image in my memory. When I saw her for the first time, we spoke about many things. She told me her father was in the Spanish battalion and that he came to visit her and her mother from time to time, and she said she was a student at the Spanish school. We agreed on a first work session. In it, she appeared to be too serious for her age. While in the studio, she asked permission to look at the portraits and the models I had painted. So I took out my large cardboard portfolio and began to show her what I had painted. She gave each painting a neutral look, occasionally concentrating more on some of them. After a while, she asked me about the position I wanted her to take, so I asked her to undress completely, then sit on a chair, cross her legs, and put one arm behind the chair. She did not hesitate for a moment to do what I requested. Despite my experience in the subject, my breathing began to quiver as I looked at her well-proportioned body disposing of the last piece of cloth scratching its transparency. In that period, I used to strive to perfectly imitate the features, the lines, and the joints. When a body was of a marvelous formation, it usually helped me in bringing out the bends, the curves, and the windings and I hardly needed to add or imagine anything outside it. However, Joséo used to insist that I should pay attention to what the model did not divulge by her corporeal appearance so that I might reach the unseen aspects hidden behind the mystery of relationships drawing us to other creatures. I did not very well understand the significance of his advice but, through Ghaylana's body, I felt that invisible element that the neutral look could not comprehend. My hand began to tremble as I traced the primary outlines of her figure. In order to conceal my agitation, I adjusted Ghaylana's position on the chair more than once and, while doing so, my hands perhaps unconsciously dwelt on touching the curve of her breasts and the smoothness of her legs. I was surprised to hear her ask in a sharp tone, "Is your mind set on painting or just fooling around?"

I did not prolong that first session and apologized for feeling tired all of a sudden. During the following sessions, I was able to control the rushing of blood in my veins and surrendered to a long dialogue with the body that played havoc with my feelings and disturbed the order of my life that had been content with the customs of the climate I spoke to you of. The first thing I thought of was to integrate Ghaylana within the group of friends so that our relationship might develop in a natural way and I could remain continuously near this woman who had awakened unfamiliar feelings in me. She said to me that I had to persuade her mother to let her go out with our group in the evening. Her mother was a frank woman of strong personality who loved her daughter and acted in collusion with her in order not to deprive her of the pleasures of youth. After reminding me that her husband was serving in the Spanish army and that he was an intractable man who could not be humored, she said to me, "I'm going to trust you because you were brought up by the Christians and know the value of women. Consider Ghaylana to be your sister, God bless you."

I reassured her and emphasized that I would take care of her more than I do of myself. I remember now that all my feelings were kindled by the biting fire of Ghaylana's eyes, motions, and

smiles and by the curves of her naked body carved in my imagination and my fingers. I wanted to have this young woman, by
any means. I could not bear to let her be far from me after she had
planted tension in my whole being and aroused all my senses.
Through her, through her body and words, through her steps, I
might be able to possess something I lacked that, alone, was what
would extinguish the burning blaze within me if I were to return
to life without anxiety as I used to be.

What I'm telling you now, Fatima, was not so clear in my
mind and feelings at the time, because he who is on the scene of
action cannot control his acts and impulses by words, and because
I did not then have the relative awareness I now have that allows
me to color things and circumstances and to organize them, although they may have been—when they occurred—nothing but
ordinary events void of this meaning I am trying to bestow on
them. This is not because the matter is related to your mother but
rather because this relationship that ties me to you now (and I
can't describe it, for it's still fresh) makes me look at my past life as
though it had a significance that would justify to this self now
talking to you its own existence in a discourse having its own
specificity. The point is not to tell you about your mother and
how I came to know her, nor is it about that period which I
made rosy by speaking to you about international Tangier, its
nightlife, and the glitter of those living in comfort. That's not
what interests me. What interests me is to talk about my self or
rather my selves that continued to run on the edges of the
shadow, within the areas of light/shade, in the midst of the mazes
of consciousness without capturing what actually formed their
essence. Continuous images and scenes but not a single one cor-
responding with an essence. Between you and me lies time, Fa-

tima, and that's what makes me not know what sound I am the echo of. You've awakened that dormant illusion which draws me anew to the whirlpool and lures me to invent some meaning for the days I lived as if my heart were a veil. Who said, "When we think we live, we are dead. And when we begin living, we are on the brink of extinction"? You and I are of different ages but it seems to me that questions of life and death join us together.

Only now have I become aware that I discovered woman in bed, through the joys of the body, in the festival of clownish physical movements: I discovered her denuded from whispers, embellishments, ornaments, and sighs of infatuation . . .

Ghaylana was the one who introduced me to the game of love, at least to the game of flirtation and ambiguous words, and of special gestures and looks that stir one's deep sorrows. Since experiencing life with her, I've come to imagine there is love in every warm intimate meeting I have with a woman; and that's perhaps because I've reached the stage of countdown on my way to extinction. But the specificity of emotions is, I now think, the justifying factor on which we depend to justify our love for life and for continuing to live it.

Let me return to my story with Ghaylana. Where have we left it? Oh, I remember: at the beginning of my attachment to her during the time I painted her. I tried many times to incite her jealousy by telling her about my love adventures, imaginary and real, in Spain and Tangier. But she took what I told her with a smile that hardly changed, saying, "You're lucky." Then she asked permission to stop the painting for a while in order to take a bite from a chocolate, with some pleasure, as I almost devoured her with my eyes. She came very near to me and put the chocolate next to my mouth; I quickly took the biggest bite I could reach, so she declared, "You're greedy." And I answered, "My greed increases with you alone. It goes beyond all limits." Then started the moment of ambiguous looks that quickly vanished when Ghaylana regained her air of pride that tormented me. Deep within, I did not want that painting to end, but she maliciously asked whether I spent the same amount of time to finish painting the other models as I did her . . .

On some days in the morning, Ghaylana brought the *churro* with her and prepared breakfast, then opened the window of my room, asking whether I did not sleep well the night before. She wove a certain intimacy between her and me to the extent she wanted and I gave myself up with astonishment to this transformation. Even my group of boon companions were astonished because I did not keep their appointments and preferred to stay with Ghaylana to watch a movie or stroll in the streets. The birthday of my friend al-Zulali was an opportune occasion to return to the tumultuous din of the group and its merriment.

After dinner, we went to a dance hall situated on the way to the mountain (I think it has now become a domed villa with green tiles that one sees at the beginning of the upward curve). The dance hall was owned by an Italian whose son was one of our group, so he donated the evening to us and put up a sign on the door that said, "Reserved until morning." We danced, drank, sang aloud together, exchanged kisses, blows, and biting jeers. In that climate, I found what I liked in keeping company with boon companions. But when I saw Ghaylana glittering, I beat my lashes and contented myself with raising my glass in her direction. After a while, she approached me to remark that I had not asked her to dance with me, so I answered that I was about to do that. When I saw her clinging to al-Zulali as they danced, flooded

by the faint red light, I thought something had brought them together and that Ghaylana was dancing as if I were not present in
the hall. How dare she dance with al-Zulali in my presence with
such harmony and consonance? My head began to turn and I became very tense, although before that moment I used to consider
her dancing with the others an ordinary matter, because of how
often I had danced and seen others dance. Perhaps my sudden
feeling that I was thrust into a desert was what made me steal out
of the dance hall and run downhill toward the city, to my studio
where I sat in front of the unfinished painting to devour with my
eyes the features of the captivating body emanating from the lines
and shades and shining wild eyes.

You'll find romantic streaks in what I'm telling you, but I
truly can't remember those moments in any other manner. At
any rate, is memory an event we lived or is it something we lack
that gives us a feeling of missing something, so we invent it? Is
memory made up of scenes that we actually lived or do we live
them by remembering what others tell us about them? Three
years ago, I was talking with a friend and telling him about a conversation between myself and a visitor I had met in Paris at an art
exhibit called "Vienna, Capital of Modernity." I was standing in
bafflement in front of Klimt's painting called *A Pregnant Woman*. I
began to mutter: I think this painting says nothing; its beauty is in
the fact that the lines, signs, and colors meet in this woman's face
full of both allure and innocence; yet it does not point to any vision of hope or despair; and what I'm muttering is emanating
from me, not from the painting . . . I was telling my friend what
happened between myself and the visitor at the art exhibit when
he burst out laughing, then noted, "My dear al-'Ayshuni. It's I

who lived what you're telling me. It's I who related to you this event, for you have not yet visited Paris!"

I fell asleep while looking at Ghaylana's painting. I don't know how much time passed before I was awakened by Joséo's voice:"Are you ready to receive a beautiful young woman at the end of the night? What a fortunate man you are. I envy you." I woke up to find Ghaylana looking at me, with blame in her eyes mixed with anxiety. I could not answer when she asked me why I had withdrawn without telling her or anyone else. She held my hand, giving me a penetrating look straight in my eyes still burdened with vestiges of sleep and perhaps of tears. She said in Spanish, "You behave like a child, as if you don't yet understand that you're the one who interests me, not al-Zulali or the others."

I was the one who interested her, not the others—she said it with spontaneity as she put her hand on my cheek. Our eyes met, then our lips. "You're the one who interests me" is an expression I don't think I'll forget, and I don't think that anything similar to its effect on me has ever been repeated in my life afterward. All through the remaining hours of that night, I experienced feelings that made me into another person, into other persons. Not all activities and experiences are equal. The criterion for me, since that night, is the cycle of metempsychosis and rebirth, for which the self becomes a theater. The criterion is the fact of being attracted to a dream, which has been latent within rays of light drawing you to a point you have not seen earlier, a dream that makes you realize that this is what should have actually been and that, without it, you'll return to the region of the living dead.

I claim I did not return to the world of the living dead until several years had passed, during which I was immersed in introspection and in exploring the world with Ghaylana and through her. My relations with my surroundings changed as if things that had been dormant and stored away somewhere woke up suddenly to take me to a labyrinthian space whose threshold I feared to cross but whose lure fascinated me, so I entered it in search of a promised happiness. And here began the journey of filling my nostrils with the scent of the beloved's body, the journey of getting accustomed to her features seemingly different every day, the journey of being careful to synchronize the rhythm of our two bodies and temperaments, the journey of being aware of details and listening to the pulse of our two hearts. Shall I say that a small gate laid open before me a nebulous universe whose riddles I had never thought of, and so I became charged with great tension that urged me to look at everything with a new eye as if I were recreating all that surrounded me and rearranging it according to an unprecedented order? Ghaylana lived our experience in a different way: she listened well when I dreamed aloud, arrived in time for agreed appointments, read a little, sang, and granted me love at every moment. She never asked me about the future of our relationship. She lived it as it was, with her bodily effervescence, in hours of tenderness and communication, in night loafing and waiting for the paintings I would complete that I felt were about to be born. I divided my time between painting, reading, and love. Joséo had arranged everything before his death: he bequeathed to me his house and an amount of money deposited in the bank, from whose interest I lived, and he also bequeathed love for painting and life. The concerns of daily life no longer preoccupied me and I had a strong feeling that I was destined to create masterpieces. All that my heart felt induced me to follow up what stirred in my depths. I used to take several months to complete a painting, only to realize in the last stage that the effort I exerted had not led to anything but the discovery of what I should avoid when painting a new painting. It was an endless toil to approach a painting hovering in my mind whose lines I could hardly get hold of. I always feel that I return to point zero.

I was at al-Ghanduri's restaurant—do you remember it? You and I had dinner there a week ago—I was there with Ghaylana for lunch. It was the end of March and the sun was gradually gathering the warmth of spring. We ate fresh fish and drank white wine that increased our ecstasy. I was distracted as I looked across the sea as if I were listening to something. After a while, in order to make me speak, as she usually did, Ghaylana asked, "What's with you, lad?" I did not answer, so she added, laughing and quoting words from a song, "What's the matter with the artist? What's the matter with him? What suddenly occurred, what happened to him?"

I took her by the hand and we walked on the pebbles till we reached the water and then I asked her to take off her shoes like me. We waded into the sea until our feet were covered above the ankles. I bent down to collect some small stones of various shapes and ran my fingers over them to feel their smoothness as if they were precious gems. Ghaylana was doing likewise and her face glowed with happiness. Then I began to speak as though to myself. I asked whether she felt the transparency of the water, the smooth polish of the stones, and the rhythm of the wings of the seagulls as they flew to and fro almost touching the water . . .

"All the things that my sight now falls on engross me as I try to fathom their various shapes and I am at a loss to give them independent existence in the painting I'll paint. You're beside me walking barefoot on this shore, yet I see you there in the distance coming out like a nymph from the folds of the waves or like a bird in the size of a cloud flying upward toward the sky. I see colors: rose, crimson, light blue, azure, light red, coral-red. I see scattered spots of light in geometric forms free of the sharpness of lines. I see that which we both see together, but through it I see scenes stored up in memories of my childhood in the village that I've not gone back to since coming to Tangier with my mother. I'm trying to organize my feelings, Ghaylana, in order to express to you what I've been feeling since the moment we sat to have lunch together on the terrace of this restaurant. Right from the first moment, I felt I was besieged all at once and thrust into what resembled a maze, and I was gradually enveloped by a veil that turned me into another person."

After a moment of silence, Ghaylana said, "Why do you complicate things and torment yourself? Paint as you've always done. I'll not be jealous of your models and will even find them for you."

I stopped speaking. I stretched out my arms toward her to embrace her as I sank further into the region of that anxiety which usually beset me whenever I contemplated how I experienced painting and forms and, perhaps in a disguised way, my relationship with Ghaylana. Five years of such life took me to another shore and sowed within me the seeds of a lifestyle different from that of most of those who surrounded me. It became basic for me to create paintings that responded to the conflicting feelings that chased me within the whirlpool. While strongly drawn to nourish my love for Ghaylana, I continued to dig for what disturbed me as I searched for a specific style. Only dialogue with what I read about the experiences of artists and writers satisfied me. Ghaylana did not understand this aspect of my experience, so our agreement was embodied in matters of pastime and entertainment. I spent long hours painting and reading, then contacted Ghaylana and went out with her to dance halls and bars to meet friends and to enjoy the fascinating nights of Tangier. We had our whims too. I remember that sexual desire took hold of us once as we were returning from dancing, so we entered a building and surrendered to the passion of our bodies on the stairs. At the climax of sex, an old French man entered. He was the owner of an antique furniture shop. He saw us panting in frenzy. As he went up the stairs, he began saying, "Oh, oh . . . Ce n'est pas vrai. This is incredible. You could at least have lain on the tiled floor. It's clean and made of expensive marble . . . This way you'll be very tired . . ."

Another time, we had lunch in the forest of the diplomatic neighborhood, then sat on the grass in the shade of a tree. We then had a short nap and when we woke up, sexual desire woke up in us too; so we went into a lavender thicket and blended together in intimate intercourse feeding on the warmth of sleep still hanging in our eyes. I still remember the smell of the soil in my nostrils as I lay on my belly after sex, listening to the rhythm of my blood slowly returning in my veins. Did the incident remind me of the smell of hot bread just out of the oven, mixed in my imagination with the smell of thyme, sesame, and olive oil?

Ghaylana interrupted her education because her father did not allow her to go to Madrid to continue her studies, so she found employment in a travel agency. After five years of our relationship, she once said to me, "My mother asked: Will al-'Ayshuni marry you?" I said to her, "Did you tell her that al-'Ayshuni is not like all the other people and that the life we now live is better than marriage?"

She was silent. She wrapped herself in her pride and since then did not return to the subject. I used to persuade myself that I had what was more important than marriage and that I was realizing a great transformation in my artistic experience, everything besides that being capable of waiting. "You're destined to something extraordinary," I used to repeat to myself with pride every morning before the mirror. I paid no attention to the changes taking place around me. Even the declaration of independence and the return of Tangier to the fold of the kingdom in 1958 did not take me out of the circle of my concerns and my rituals of love and life. I was content with my own kingdom, reckless in my contemplations and allurement.

Suddenly Ghaylana stopped visiting me. Three days passed and she did not come. Then a week passed and I did not see her. I began to wonder about this absence. I contacted her at work and was told she no longer worked at the travel agency. I tried to ask about her at home and noticed her father sitting on a chair by the door. It was his custom to do that after he had retired from the Spanish army the year before. I continued trying to track her but did not succeed for several weeks. Only then did I begin to think I might have lost Ghaylana. What if she disappeared? What if she died? I was assailed by conjectures but realized that Ghaylana was part of a larger scheme, which is this kingdom that I had created for myself from illusions, dreams of creative ability, communication with nature, and worship in the temple of love and sex. She might have been behind this transformation but I began to feel that my transformation had reached a stage that created its own defense against storms and tribulations. I was overtaken by a nameless sorrow. I sought help in painting and wine, and a strong tendency developed in me to avoid many things needed in daily life and its pleasures. I let my beard grow and immersed myself in melancholy.

After several weeks, when the summer was just beginning, I was walking one evening on Boulevard Pasteur, lost among crowds of different faces as though seeking to cheer myself up and get rid of boredom. I looked at the faces, hardly distinguishing between them. They were a noisy mass that made the walk an entertaining game, especially for young people excelling in rubbing shoulders with one another and making flirtatious passes. I saw her with her mother, so I stopped without much ceremony. She caught sight of me, smiled, and turned to her mother to whisper a few words before approaching me. We shook hands and exchanged greetings. Words came out of me as though I were not the one who said them. She explained that she had gotten married and would go to Fez with her bridegroom at the end of the month. She said there was no way out of that because her father had approved the marriage. Her mother's voice urged her to hurry up, so she apologized, wished me a happy life, then turned away, thrusting herself among the crowds coming and going.

I continued my distracted walk among the masses of male and female summer vacationists who were happy to stroll in the noisy, crowded street. I walked while the five-year film rolled in my mind. That "ending" soon appeared to me natural, for I did not want marriage and Ghaylana could no longer resist her family more than she had done. The experience, no doubt, had exhausted itself as far as she was concerned. She was no longer able to keep up with the artist's ego in that logic which led to nothing. I began to realize that I had to settle for solitude and try its most extreme cases. In this veranda facing the sea, I passed many nights awake, drowned in utter silence, while above me were worlds that could not be confined by sight, space, or darkness. While contemplating, my whole life appeared to me void of meaning, more like a cat's scratches in piles of hay or like the chirping of cicadas on a summer night. But I continued to paint and read. Then, motivated by curiosity, I made bold to organize an exhibit of my paintings. I was surprised that my old friends came on the opening day, with indications of joy and pride written all over them. Journalists gathered around me seeking declarations and interviews, while I was almost a stranger in that field. However, I did my best to cull my words from what I had stored up during my readings and contemplations. During that exhibit, I became acquainted with al-Dahmani, the owner of the gallery in the capital, with whom we had dinner last week. Since then, he has continued to come to me to buy my paintings, sometimes even buying what I had not yet finished. During that exhibit, I became acquainted also with Kanza, a young woman from Marrakesh who had come to spend the summer holiday in Tangier. She entered the gallery one morning and found me reading what the visitors had written in a large book I had placed on a table to collect their reactions. She went around for a while from one painting to another, then she came to me and asked for the painter. I smiled and pointed to myself. She began to speak freely about her impressions and her admiration of the naked models "because they brought out the beauty of the Moroccan woman whose value was not fairly recognized." She then rambled aimlessly, but her Marrakesh dialect gave her chatter a special flavor. What appealed to me was that she was plucky and made you sense her personality in no uncertain terms. I don't say she was beautiful but her way of expressing herself and her self-confidence brought out a character worthy of attention. Our conversation was protracted, so I suggested that we have dinner together in order to continue what we had begun and to have an opportunity to strengthen our relationship. She told me that she was employed in the government office of the Ministry of Traditional Crafts, that she had graduated from the College of Law and now lived by herself after being divorced by her husband, who was addicted to drinking and who often insulted and assaulted her, and she kept repeating, "We had no marriage at all."

With Kanza, I had a relationship that was tantamount to a warrior's rest. Between me, on the one hand, and things and people, on the other, there was a distance that limited my heart's chaos. She had just come out of a hellish experience and was seeking nothing but to live in freedom, even if that required a behavior of maneuver and dissimulation on her part. We understood each other on many things and so our relationship became an element of balance for both of us. We began exchanging visits: she came to Tangier and I went to Marrakesh; and every time, we invented the format and the details of each meeting. She was interested in culture and art, and she liked to discuss with me problems of creativity that I faced. She wanted me to organize other art exhibits and integrate myself in cultural life so as to occupy a place that was congruent with what she thought I deserved. I understood her logic but was not enthusiastic about it, for I was not desirous of fame, especially because I used to hear about the conflicts among the artists. She suggested that I should come and live in Marrakesh for a few months; perhaps I would find in its atmospheres responses to the anxieties that disturbed me. Residing in Marrakesh appealed to me because, during my previous visits, I felt I lacked something essential and that made me feel I was almost a stranger in my own country. Whenever I heard a piece of a colloquial poem set to traditional music, or whenever I listened to a Berber song or a tribal ballad of the al-Awz district, or whenever I saw an *Awash* dance . . . during my encounters with the folk music of the South, my heart pounded surprisingly and my body felt numb as I went into something similar to a trance. I often wondered: How could I belong to this country if I did not identify with all that made up its depth and the very atoms of its soil? I did not want my relation to the other regions of my country to remain an external one, a relation of a tourist discovering its exotic tunes. I wanted to feel the same thrill as the people's when listening to a mountain ballad or when enjoying Andalusian music, with which I had a longer experience. A philosophizing friend I came to know during one of my visits to Rabat would say, "It is the return of what has been repressed." But I was actually living the state of rupture on the physical level too, for I could not tolerate being distant from certain elements that I felt were surrounding me and shaking all my being. I was anxious to contain the totality of atmospheres that secretly inhabited my emotional life and made me recognize them in my surroundings.

Let me summarize what happened: I lived in Marrakesh for several months, during which I was withdrawn from social life and was content with my relationship with Kanza. I roamed through the South, opening my eyes to its light and colors, listening with ecstasy to its music and language, seeking inspiration from its universe in whatever I painted or made first outlines of. My relationship with Kanza had an organized character about it. Our two bodies discovered the extent of their agreement and I was very pleased with our evening privacy and conversations.

She tried to make me take part in her political activities, but she did not find any desire on my part to do that. I followed the same path that had been established in my behavior: I listened well to what took place around me, but I found no pleasure in giving myself the illusion that I could change the order of things. I neither wanted to be a witness nor a struggler in the process of change. Yet deep inside, I was not an onlooker. I was attracted to my inner world and looked for a broader vision. Was it an illusion of mine? Perhaps. I did not want to be an intruder in a situation in which I did not feel I was totally immersed with my whole being and in complete harmony with what I was doing. I am very annoyed when I find people occupying positions in which they do not give all they can in accordance with their real conviction. That's why I preferred to remain secluded in my private realm, happy with the life of contemplation and introspection. And who knows? That may have been the cause of the sweeping feeling that took hold of me, several months after my residence in Marrakesh, that I could not live far from the sea, not from any sea but specifically from the sea of Tangier, which had left in me the strong impression that the direction of the North, across the Strait [of Gibraltar], across Spain, led to an opening, an ampleness, a wide scope, an immense extent, a vastness, a space in which things would not be as we knew them. Another illusion of mine? Perhaps. It seems to me now that my relation with Tangier crystallized during the time I was far away from it: a relation of someone who desired, who was in an ordeal, who wanted the city to devour him because it alone could awaken passion in the pores of his body, in the paths of his soul. It is difficult for us to invent a city as we would wish, for it also defines our imaginings and our movements inside its space. The city is not an absolute place, for in it we live an unseen dialectic between body and space, between a place that transcends and a time that circumscribes.

After my residence in Marrakesh, I did not return to the Tangier that I am now coloring for you through my illusions. I rather returned to a space that I felt had changed and whose history in my memory was stronger than it was in the places and repeated scenes of my daily life. Perhaps you notice that I take protection in the life I've lived in Tangier for fifty years and that I cling to it and don't want to see any other. Nonetheless, the city lives its own present with confidence and with indifference to my nostalgic yearnings. I've had to learn how to open my eyes and ears to absorb all that happens in it; and the city has likewise opened its memory equally to all events, temperaments, and histories. But can we really get hold of what is happening in it?

Toward the end of the 1960s, two years—I think—after my return from Marrakesh, I saw Ghaylana again. I was returning from Spain across the Strait of Gibraltar. I saw her on board the ship: she was wearing a yellow dress and a navy blue hat with a very wide brim, and her embellishing cosmetic powders did not succeed in concealing the ravages of time. The sharpness of her wild eyes, however, declared her to be the Ghaylana I knew. She rushed to me and kissed me in a spontaneous manner: "Hello to our great artist. It has been years I've not seen you . . ." She was elegant, continuously smiling, mixing Spanish and Arabic. Had I not known her, I would have thought she was a model, one of those women we see on the pages of glossy journals advertising Madame Rochas's perfume: the symbol of femininity at a mature age! She spoke about her life since getting married and I measured the passage of time through her words. Were things moving

around me while I was motionless? Her marriage lasted about
ten years. At first she was happy, she said, with the rituals of living
in old Fez with her husband—your father—who "reared the
young ones and traded the old ones" (I asked her to explain and
she said that he was a merchant who made profit from buying
and selling sheep and calves). He treated her well and loved her in
his own way but the life of calm and the burden of traditions suffocated her. You were five years old when she requested that they
separate, remaining two lovers as when they had first met. He
asked her what she would do after divorce and she said she would
return to Tangier because she missed the sea and the east wind
that changed one's temperament, she missed having tea at
Madame Porte's tearoom and the din of the promenade on
Boulevard Pasteur . . . She said a few things and he guessed the
rest. Ghaylana was in need of larger space because the seed of
wanderlust was dying in her veins. He made it a condition to
have custody of you, Fatima, the one who carried within her the
quintessence of the two contradictory temperaments.

IN that meeting, Ghaylana spoke to me in detail about her present. She said that she was returning from Madrid, where she was
working. I asked what kind of work she was doing and she said,
"I'm now working on my own. At the beginning, I was inexpe-
rienced and did not see through the scheme of the procurer who
offered to take me to Madrid to work with him in a restaurant.
He had arranged everything to trap me. After my return from Fez
to Tangier, I felt I was a stranger and my mother did not relish the
story of my divorce. Money had become everyone's goal. Salvation for me was associated with going to Spain. In Madrid, I
found dozens of Moroccan women of all kinds and classes work-

ing in bars, restaurants, and dance halls, and selling their bodies. It was a flourishing and profitable emigration of bodies whose inducement was difficult to resist. And that was the project that the procurer forced me to enter. So I decided to become rich and learn all the secrets of the profession in order to make money that would secure a good life in Tangier for my daughter and myself. I'm not responsible for morality, my beloved artist. I say this especially after the secrets of respectable men, here and there, surprised me when I gradually discovered them. I want to send my daughter abroad to study and I want to gain the respect of others through what I possess, for this is the prevailing measuring rod of respect today. While practicing prostitution, I'm now shouldering all my responsibilities. It even seems to me that I can publicly announce: I'm a prostitute with premeditation. What do you think of that, my dear artist?"

Deep inside, I found myself agreeing with what she had done. I took her hand and kissed it, as though the span of time she was speaking about did not separate us.

She continued, "My situation improved in the last three years. Franco's death was beneficial to me, because Spanish morality was liberated from its former staid shackles after he passed away. Prostitutes came to have a recognized legal status and I was able to reject the procurer's guardianship. I now live in an apartment on Goya Street. My telephone number is in the entertainment brochure that anyone who likes may buy from the newsstands, and in it I advertise myself as Zahiya, the professional name I chose for myself: 'Zahiya, from the country of sunshine, is at your service at all times with talent and sincerity—massage, conviviality, humor, drinking companionship, striptease . . . provided the client's age is not less than sixty years.' "

It was as though Ghaylana were speaking about another woman, but she did not conceal that she was pleased with her new personality. She added, "A year ago, I placed a special advertisement in the grand hotels frequented by wealthy Arabs. I sought the help of one of the teachers at Ibn Khaldun Secondary School to write an advertisement in an attractive Arabic form. The colloquial text was printed under the photograph of myself, naked, and it said: 'I'm here, at your service. I'm a chocolate in your hands. Suck me in your mouth and suck me again. You'll find me to be a gem. I'll melt in your mouth and sucking brings me back to life. I'm here, at your service . . . ' "

I shouted, "Good! This is real creativity. What were the results?"

"Satisfactory," she said. "Last year I bought a villa on Tetuan Road. My daughter Fatima will graduate from the university this year and I'm looking for a commercial project to invest my savings in. Youth does not last, you know. I was constantly thinking of you but I know that our paths are different."

WE spent that night together.

On the next day, I invited her to lunch at al-Ghanduri's restaurant. She shook her head and smiled, "I suspect you're a partner with the restaurant's owner and you're hiding it from me, aren't you?"

The water, the stones, the sun were all there, exactly as they had been twenty years ago. But I did not ask her to take off her shoes and I did not think of the colors and lines and of what would give life to my paintings. She told pleasant stories about her life and work in Madrid, and she did not appear to be troubled or to be having two minds about herself. She spoke as though her life were a natural development, a mask like other masks, no one being better than anyone else. I thought to myself that the time we spent together had its unforgettable specificity, but it was not everything, at least as far as she was concerned, clinging to her projects and profitable work as I found her to be. When we parted, she promised to visit me every time she returned from Madrid.

THAT evening, I wrote in my notebook: "At al-Ghanduri's restaurant, I felt at first that Ghaylana and I were resuming our interrupted relationship. But her vanished innocence and her new personality drew my attention to the fact that many possibilities do also exist in reality. Matters are not as I used to imagine: that one possesses the world either through money and power or through internal adoption of values renouncing material things. No, there is more than one possibility and the motives are difficult to classify. There is also the issue of beguiling the power of time. Can we possess it, can we tame it? Is our problem always with time? What direction in life brings us nearer to its reality? "
       Since that meeting, she has not visited me in three years—I believe. What shall I tell you more, Fatima?

I don't calculate life in years, nor do I measure profit by what I achieve but rather by those few moments that flash in a special way, shaking our human existence, casting us beyond what is familiar, and engraving love for life in our heart of hearts. These are moments that don't often recur. I remember that I experienced one of them during the time I lived with Ghaylana. I had just finished one of my paintings and stood in front of it to contemplate it. Something that I had often imagined in my mind was there in it and I saw it. Moments later, Ghaylana came and we embraced, then the bed enfolded us. Never has my body been ablaze as it was that evening. I felt I was a symphony, whose strings the players awakened to the point of madness.

After that, we sat here on the veranda, drinking gin and tonic and wrapped in deep silence. Suddenly, I was seized by joy, by something moving inside me, creeping like a spring, filling me like a doll about to jump off its seat. I began to shout, "Hold me down, I'm about to fly; please hold me down, I'm not joking." Ghaylana rushed and held me down as I continued to repeat, "Joy is about to make me fly." Never will I forget that moment. This condition lasted several days, during which I used to walk in the streets with fear that I would fly. For all people, I felt love; and to all, I spoke with affection . . . Something that can't be believed by anyone who has not experienced it.

The source of my misery now is that I miss those moments. I feel as though nothing is happening, as though the experience I am living now, I have lived before. I don't deny that your visit has thrilled me and awakened joy in me, but the burden of age limits the vehemence of my response.

Was it possible for my life to take another path? I don't regard that as unlikely, but what's the use of my life being different from what it actually is? And what's the use of the world being different too? Will that mean there will not be someone who will be fascinated by truth, by art, by running after what he imagines to be the essence of things?

MY journey has taken a long time while I was searching for the mysteries of being and nonbeing, and for the alchemy that bestows transparency on what we daily coexist with. My puzzlement increases and with it my questions accumulate. I've followed the achievements of the abstract artists and the imagists, I've dwelled long in front of the works of modernism and futurism, and in front of others clad in metaphysics and mythology, I've walked in the steps of avant-gardism and realism . . . But all these paths vanish and only specific paintings remain, through which shine the names of Rembrandt, Cézanne, Braque, Monet, Klee, Matisse, Giacometti, Picasso, Dubuffet . . . I'm scattered among all that I see and all that I introspect. I feel I'm lost and all those masterpieces can hardly help me. I try to make light of things and say my escape is to exploit all this to my benefit. But I often feel that I'm crushed under the weight of this beautiful legacy. It's not sufficient for me to say like others that technique is universal and that I should begin to create from the point where the forerunners have left off. The crack is deeper than I imagined. In the beginning, in my phase of innocence, I painted with indifference, I painted as I breathed; the outcome of experience, reading, and self-discovery now paralyzes me and controls my movements and my every breath. I now suffer a lot before I am able to draw a single painting that moves one's imagination and excites one's pleasure. I know one thing and that is that I should continue painting, but I am sure of nothing. Everything seems to be confused and nebulous. I don't even claim I've chosen this path and this situation. Never have I talked to anyone earlier with such spontaneity and yet I hardly know you. I say I know you and I don't know you. I talk to you and I don't know of what people and of what sounds I am the echo.

3

If you do not expect the unexpected,
you will never reach the truth.
—*By a writer whose name slipped my mind*

AL-'AYSHUNI WAS LYING DOWN on his back on a pongee quilt,
completely naked under the scorching sun flooding the veranda.
It was about five o'clock and he had not yet had his lunch. He
had been trying to work on an unsuccessful painting, whose internal rhythm he could not control. He had woken up late and
out of sorts after a noisy night spent at a nocturnal dance hall that
offered a long musical program by a number of songstresses from
al-Shawiyya district. He found himself caught up in a nightclub
evening party when he accidentally met a friend to whom he
had been introduced in Marrakesh and whom he had not seen
for years. "You're a godsend to keep me company," the friend had
said. "We'll spend the evening with Sundusiyya, the songstress
from al-Shawiyya. Her voice is a mixture of black earth and
wheat flavor, my dear artist."

The dance hall was as crowded as resurrection day: those
standing were more than those seated, bodies were sweating and
oozing the beer, the whisky, the gin, and the wine imbibed.

Screams, laughs, open flirtation. Even his friend began to scream after the third glass, "O Sundusiyya! I offer you my life." She favored him with special looks in which affection blended with coyness, her beauty shining proudly despite the beginnings of creeping old age. Perhaps it was "mature femininity," as the ambiguity that shrouds the faces of certain women at such an age is usually called. She appeared to be past fifty. She stood in the middle of six young women in their prime. Holding the baton, she swayed with dignity, her oblong dark face and her quiet and wide, honey-colored eyes endowing the scene with a special character. "Look, listen, and consider deeply," his friend whispered to him. "The likes of this songstress are few. Forget the young dolls standing with her. She's their lady superior. Look at the swaying of her belly and the fire of her voice, and judge their effect . . ." From time to time, he gave him a verbal picture of Sundusiyya in the prime of her life and said, "I'd like you to have known her twenty years ago when she was in her prime in Stat. She captivated everyone's mind. Whenever I had time, I came to listen to her . . . Those were good old days." He then screamed again, "O Sundusiyya! I offer you my life." And he sang with her passages of the songs she was singing from time to time. The voice of a client rose in imitation of the screams of al-'Ayshuni's friend: "I'll join the army for your sake." Laughs rang out and the beautiful songstress could not help smiling.

At three o'clock in the morning, al-'Ayshuni felt he was drunk despite his moderation in drinking. He was beset by memories and sorrows, and he felt he was suffocating in the midst of the noise and the screams in the muggy heat. He asked to be excused but his friend retained him for a short while, then saw him off at the door, saying he would stay in the dance hall until Sundusiyya finished her performance.

Lying on his back and staring at the sky distractedly, al-'Ayshuni hardly stopped at a thought or a memory. From time to time, he closed his eyes to avoid the rays of the sun and keep its light glowing behind his eyelids. At that moment, dozens of fantasies and forms figured before his closed eyes, then faded away to be replaced by others in a quick, intertwining montage. A short while ago, he had been engrossed in the difficult outlines of his painting, whose signs and spaces he wanted to be characterized by a transmutation of humans into animals: crowded, broad faces whose looks and formations revealed their animality. This graphic idea suggested itself to him on reading a book on the Aztec art of Mexico, in which he saw pictures of the gods of fertility, the earth, the soil, jewelry, and the wind . . . then the picture of a statue of an animalized man. He said, "Perhaps this will help me personify the confused feelings that often beset me, making me feel I am outside my humanness and letting me look at others through an animality that colors my vision of them." When he was drawing his sketches, he did not want them to come out in a familiar form: a man's face fitted on an animal's body, because that would remove certain essential features of his confused experience. So he tried to borrow animal heads and fit them on human bodies, disfiguring their eyes to let them acquire an absolute animality by losing words and looks. Despite that, he was not satisfied with what he outlined because, after executing it, the form appeared independent of what he had intended. Those animals remained humanized so that, if they talked, they would say what resembled familiar speech. No, this was not what he wanted. He put his pencil and papers aside, and he went to the veranda, to the sea, protecting his eyes with his hands from the rays of impudent light blinding his sight.

While he was at the threshold of a slow-coming nap, just before sleep blurred his eyes, he heard the doorbell ring at the pressure of some hurried hand. He put on his robe before opening the door, to be faced with an unexpected surprise: Ghaylana in a yellow traditional gown, her unveiled face revealing the ravages of time upon the formerly beautiful woman. Perhaps her carob-colored eyes with their vivid sparkle still preserved some of her attractiveness, but her wrinkled face, lacking its former comeliness, swept away her enchanting looks. Before he could embrace her, she said many things about his laziness and his ingrained bad habits of relaxation and solitude. He said to her, "It's been a long time . . . What's with you, have you forgotten my address, woman?" She protested, "Call me Hajja, please. Hajja Ghaylana." Hardly able to suppress laughing, he said, "The more, the merrier. No objection to that, Lalla Hajja Ghaylana. May it be a blessed pilgrimage."

Three years had passed since he had last seen her. He could hardly believe it. She had then still been beautiful, overflowing with vivacity, exciting the devils of sex lurking in his body when they both had lunch together at al-Ghanduri's restaurant. What did this gravity do other than hasten the settling of old age in her body? He asked her about this sudden change and she answered that he was not qualified to judge whether her behavior was sudden or not, because he lived far from the daily life of people, exclusively occupying himself with his art and confidentially talking to the nymphs of the sea, not bothering to ask about her for it was her duty to come to him. "Is this love?" she asked. "But

I know you," she continued. "Since the time you left me when I was in the prime of youth, love, and dreams, I realized that I had to find my own way alone, whatever the price. I'm not afraid of enduring humiliation and the whims of instincts. But I refuse to be a burden to you, to hamper your progress, for you are the one I loved more than anyone else."

Al-'Ayshuni felt that what Ghaylana was saying was more than reproach. A wounded woman was speaking. Many worlds separated them, and the old familiarity had become a curtain preventing him from guessing what Ghaylana had gone through in her real-life experiences, continuously open to all possibilities.

He fell silent. He tried to protect himself by silence but was surprised when Ghaylana asked him to pour her a glass of whisky. She sipped her drink, again and again, audibly taking pleasure in each sip. Then she said, "May God curse this time of ours. The ancients said it right: 'Go along with time in its cycle, and laugh with the monkey when it is in a good disposition.'"
And she wondered, what else could she have done in order to deflect her past and be assimilated with the inhabitants of her neighborhood but go on pilgrimage, wear the traditional gown, and, from time to time, offer charity dinners in which eulogies of the Prophet [Muhammad] were sung? What was in one's heart, however, only God Most High knew. In her case, she knew her heart was good and wished everyone well, despite the bad times she had fallen on. She did not renounce her past but was proud of it because, thanks to her body, she could—on her own—discover the life she did not know, and she was able to experience people and save money to buy a villa and secure a better future for her daughter.

At this point in her story, al-'Ayshuni became aware that a

lament began to envelope her tone of voice as she asked what he thought of what her daughter Fatima had done, having left a year ago without leaving any indication of her whereabouts. She had not even sent a single letter and had not asked about her own little daughter, whom she had left with her father in Fez. All the hopes that Ghaylana had pinned on her daughter Fatima were now sunk in the sands of frivolity because of her rash behavior, despite the fact that she, her mother, had not been remiss in treating her well, even giving her absolute freedom, and she had pleaded with her to continue her studies in Spain, France, or any other country of her choice. What was it that changed Fatima? She no longer knew what went through her head and mutual understanding between them was soon lost. "What could I have done more than that? Even her marriage was not in accordance with my will. And after she was divorced, she took her daughter to her father to take care of her, and she continued her life in the same manner, hardly settling down to anything. Her father, my former husband, did not bring her to account or interfere in her affairs either. I suffer alone, because the hopes I had pinned on her have quickly collapsed and left me shaken on the waters . . . How happy you must be, artist, for not having a child and not having to endure being attached to a creature of your own flesh and blood."

After a pause, al-'Ayshuni said, "It's your fault. You could have brought her to Tangier when you left Fez. Perhaps I would have taken charge of her and attended to her upbringing."

Ghaylana laughed aloud, "This talk is new. I won't believe it until I see it."

"No, no. This is a simple matter. I love children and I think I can take the role of father. The fact that I never married has nothing to do with the headache of children's upbringing. And in order to convince you, I suggest that we act a family scene in which we imagine Fatima's presence with us. Let's begin. You take her role as well as your own. Let's say it is seven o'clock in the evening and I've just returned from the Customs, where I work as an accountant."

Al-'Ayshuni gets up and goes to the door. He opens it, then slams it violently, "Ghaylana, come, take the bag."

She hurries to him, "Welcome home." She tries to kiss him on his cheek but he shoves her away, looking angrily at the low-cut neckline of her dress.

"This lack of modesty does not appeal to me. God has commanded modest cover."

Taken aback, she says, "You're exaggerating. I'm at home. I'm not outside, with a stranger. Come in first and rest before you begin to shout and yell."

"Whenever I talk to you, you deny what I observe about you. And then there is that Fatima and her evil deeds, where's she?"

Trying to alter her voice, Ghaylana says, "Yes, father. I'm here studying my lessons."

"Come here. The grocer tells me that a certain young man walked you home to the doorstep."

"Yes, father. That's Hamid and he's with me at school. He too is going to sit for the *baccalauréat*."

"I don't like my daughter to go with boys. The world is a hodgepodge. And today's young people are all up to devilish deeds."

"No, dad. He comes from a good family. And his father is an employee in the electric company."

"Good families are those with the big scandals. Didn't you

hear the other day about the female students arrested at the Cinco Minutos Bar, where a Spanish journalist was taking pictures of them naked, and with him was a Moroccan, unfortunately?"

"No, father. The world has good and bad people."

"There's nothing pleasing in this world. I don't want you to mix with the young people. Pay attention to your studies, that's first and foremost." Then turning to Ghaylana, the mother, he says, "What's with you, looking at me so? You knew what was happening and you concealed it from me, didn't you?"

Ghaylana answers, "This is a new tone. There's nothing left but veiling our daughter and assigning her a guard to take her out and bring her back in."

"Let me bring up my daughter. I know what's happening these days . . ."

Ghaylana interrupted him, laughing, unable to continue acting the scene: "God bless you. I have nothing to say. At any rate, artist, you're indeed a good father. That's what Fatima needed, so that her feet should not go off the safe course."

Al-'Ayshuni said, "Perhaps that's why I didn't get married. Many things suggest to me that the prevailing model of husbands needs such presentation of authority as well as living in isolation and seeking safety. All a husband must tell himself to be safe is this: Think of food, clothing, housing, and the car; love your wife zealously and show your jealousy for her even without cause; secure nourishment for your children and bridle them because they don't know their own good; associate with persons like you who are pacific and don't interfere in politics; seek a modest life, even if the government bares your back; don't ask why you exist, for the Creator chooses the best for you; there's no harm in following the news, but you should remain an onlooker until circumstances improve and good citizens like you will be fairly treated."

He looked again at Ghaylana's face and his mind went wool-gathering. "Thirty years ago," he thought, "this was another creature who used to turn my body and soul on. But haven't I changed too? It's as if I'm looking at her from another world. For thirty years, I've been running after things shimmering in my imagination and hardly taking any form . . . They were closer to continuously renewed illusions. But refusing to become part of the routine relationships, I now feel an inhuman void. Is it because I've continued to emphasize the necessity of clinging to illusions that would give us a horizon that would save us from routine living and overwhelming reification? Yet, when illusions collapse, I find myself exposed to storms, so I change again into a stupid robot moving mechanically. We were separated thirty years ago and each of us took a different path, but I find myself still facing the same questions that motivated me to choose solitude and the adventure of painting, and to seek contemplation and the whims of the body. Am I the same man? I lived a variety of moments, I took numerous personalities, and I discovered a lot. I was ecstatic with what I learned, but I now return to meet with persons, fingerprints, and seeds of thoughts from the past, and all that changed in them and me is no more than mere features of a tragedy enveloping the paths of my journey. I look at Ghaylana now and feel I'm defeated, I'm an empty drum, with no sound or echo. I envy her for having filled this period of her life with events, persons, and experiences that colored her life and her attitudes toward what she harvested from the passage of days and nights. Yet, I'm not sure that I would have been less miserable if I had 'filled' my time with things that Ghaylana had filled her time with or with things resembling them. During my stay in Marrakesh, Kanza used to lure me into the repeated daily routine: she woke up before I did in the morning, prepared breakfast and brought it to my bed, tickled me so that I would open my eyes, filled the tub in the bathroom, placed the slippers under my feet. She asked me what suit I wanted to wear and what food I desired to eat that day, then she gave me an appointment for our meeting that evening. . . . After the rituals of dinner, we turned to reading and exchanging comments, but I quickly became aware of that excessively organized decor: the beds with their quilts of plant designs, the clean shining tables, the white drapes lined with thick wax-colored curtains . . . Everything suggested cleanliness, safety, establishment. And I began to be fidgety. The old passion, deep-seated within me, moved, and I invented excuses to go home, with the pretext that I wanted to add to the painting certain details that had just occurred to me. The truth was that I was greatly annoyed with the thought that I might become part of that decor or of any other decor.

"And when I happen to visit some of my married friends, an overwhelming desire overtakes me, a desire to live like them a patterned life with a certain organization to it, included in a common social horizon that disperses anxiety and the questionings of the fragile, apprehensive self. But I don't find myself anywhere but in the thick of chaos, on the brink of what is permanently temporary, and in the maze of solitude and wanderlust . . . Only then does my blood come back to my veins and only then does my body pulsate with its tense rhythm, and I am overwhelmed by the shades of a nameless happiness, an obscure and confused bliss encompassed by a carnival of illusions and aspirations whose warp is dream and whose woof is mythologization."

Again he looked at Ghaylana as she put ice cubes in her glass while still talking at length about her worries and her puzzlement at her daughter Fatima's silence. What could he tell her? A moment of emptiness and separation enveloped him, in which he felt in a flash something similar to a terror that suddenly peeked from its hiding place. All things, events, and faces appeared together in one place, without retouch, in a cage. They were diminutive, weightless. There was no room for expansion. Contraction beset memories, times, and spaces and transformed them into ashes. And yet, he felt an overwhelming desire to be released from the enclosure of that unexpected terror. He suddenly remembered that he had not told her about Fatima's visit to him at home, before going on her trip, so he began telling her about it. She stopped talking for a while under the influence of the surprise; then she asked how he liked her. He said she was beautiful, had a strong personality, possessed features of her mother but differed from her. She enquired about aspects of that difference and he said that Fatima was daring, that she lived without camouflage, that she defied life's difficulties. Ghaylana hit her thigh with a loud slap, objecting, "Where's the defiance you talk about, Mr. Artist? She fails in her marriage, abandons her daughter, then runs away from her country. And you say she defies? I don't understand. Perhaps you found in her that which resembles your own nature, and so you wanted to defend her. Has she been able, like me, to defy the hard circumstances I had and to achieve the tangible results I did? I didn't seek to be pampered and I didn't let others crush me. Besides, things are judged by their results. I bore all kinds of violence, I learned to be harsh, I was not afraid of experience, I suffered the degradation of my body—but I realized what I wanted and imposed my respect on others after I learned their logic . . . Does she know what she wants? Has she known anything but that she refuses the social system, its injustice and its harshness? How often have I begged her to open her eyes and see what's happening around her so that she can firmly keep her position and impose herself by completing her education and abandoning illusions of rash rebellion . . . But she was carried away by mirage-like dreams, which soon made her fall into the abyss of anxiety and daydreams, in the company of weakness and hesitation. I was fascinated by her education and her ability to speak, but I could not abandon my own experience, which had taught me that the world was not created as we wished it to be and that we should exist in it forcefully in order to be able to live, to live first, do you hear me well? After that, changes may happen, or that's what she called them. As for me, I am not concerned with changes nor to whose interest they are when they do happen. I often asked her to look at my own experience and to scrutinize its details, which I related to her quite frankly. But she persisted in her obstinacy and I got tired of her whimsical behavior and her puzzling silence. In spite of all that I did for her, she takes off and sends me no news of her, in order to increase my suffering. Put my mind to rest if you have any news of her."

She continued to drink as she talked, and her face was flushed and her eyes narrowed slightly. Al-'Ayshuni looked at her, trying to suppress a smile at the condition of Hajja Ghaylana, who was about to be drunk and appeared to him as a woman who had nothing to do with Ghaylana, the young woman he had known fifty years earlier. This woman was aggrieved, speaking with agony and anguish, and belonged to the world of people and their problems. What could he answer, knowing nothing about Fatima since her visit of the previous year, after which he had no news of her. However, he had to console her. At the same time, he was moved by this new appearance of Ghaylana who appeared more real than anything else, more real even than the room furniture and the crawling darkness of the evening. She appeared real because of the experiences she had been through, perhaps because of the fingerprints of time on her face and body. He said to himself that the result of the thirty years which they lived separately, each on a different path, was the epitome of two contradictory experiences and that, if he wanted to catch a glimpse of that lapsed time, he had inevitably to make her talk about topics that had puzzled him and caused continuous torment in his depths.

He said to her, "What does sex mean to you?"

She said, "A pleasure unequaled by any other, when it is perfect . . . But for the last twenty years, I've had sex as if I've been carrying burdens, true to God."

He did not say to her, "The sex desire enlivens our bodies, which remain dead when they are far from its allurements. It is the memory that records the history of our existence outside the duality of body and soul."

He said to her, "Haven't you ever achieved orgasm without love?"

She said, "That happened with a transient person, one evening in Madrid. I was tired, disgusted with the burdens of my profession and its mechanical movements. I dragged my body, as though it were separated from myself. I was beset by the memory of sexual pleasure in past days (with you, for example, it constituted unforgettable moments). I continued to surrender myself to memory as I sat at a summer café. Next to me sat a black man; he was handsome and was smiling to me from time to time. He then moved to my table and tried to speak English to me but I didn't understand what he said. When it was impossible for us to reach mutual understanding, his face showed signs of regret. Suddenly I felt that if I slept with him I would achieve the orgasm I had missed for a long time. I quickly held his hand and pressed it with tenderness, my eyes bright with that revealing glint. In turn, he began to look at me with responsive eyes. So I gestured and invited him to my apartment next to the café . . . And I got what I expected."

He did not say to her, "You remind me of one of Ingmar Bergman's films: The heroine was in a country whose language she did not know. She was alone and abandoned. The war was on, and she was fleeing its hell. She met him (he worked as a waiter in a café), he too came from another country and was lost and hungry. They were alone in her hotel room and the cinematic scene spoke one language only: the voice of the naked woman speaking to the body of the naked man who understood nothing of what that hungry, anguished, frightened woman said . . . She kissed every part of his body and spoke, relating all about her alienation as her body shook. He was imprisoned in his own silence and passion as she continued her raving because (it was as if) she felt that speech was necessary to reach orgasm, full orgasm, achieved also (basically?) through words and unreachable without utterance."

He said to her, "What about your relations with people?"

She said, "It seems to me they run away from something or search for something they don't know. But my profession made it incumbent on me to be one of the illusions that, they think, would provide them with what they seek. I was not allowed to have natural relations with people. I could not appear to be weak, worried, or unable to give them the pleasure they ran after. But I used to understand their loneliness and let them draw near the moments of communication when they gave up their masks. I also made it a habit of mine to make my customers a subject of entertainment by besieging them with embarrassing questions and pretending to sympathize with them in order to discover some of what lay hidden in their breasts. And there was something really entertaining there. What gives me pain, though, is my relation with my daughter Fatima: how has it gone from mutual understanding to estrangement and silence?"

He did not say to her, "There's something similar to rust that threatens our relations with the others, so that communication changes into a dialogue of the deaf, and warm emotions change to ashen complacency. Is it because collusion with the others changes our relations from neutrality to risk-taking? But rust can build up also between us and our self, which then sinks into an isolating nebulousness. Loneliness is not always a rupture that paralyzes our immediacy with the others, for it is rather harsher when it besieges us deep within and makes us a ship without a haven, an existence without certainty . . . That's why I was not surprised when Hadidesh, who worked as a guard at the Minzah Hotel, was astonished as he related to me about Barbara Hutton, the wealthy American woman who lived many years in Tangier in luxury, glory, and the uproar of parties, and yet used to say to him, when she called him to keep her company with his spontaneous conversation, 'Nobody knows how miserable I am!' He commented: 'Happiness is neither in having wealth nor in having social rank, Si 'Ayshuni; to have one's mind at rest is better than the whole world.' I did not want to make him doubt the value of a restful mind, and whether it was ever possible in this world or was simply one of those terms epitomizing complex reality that we need in order to cheat ourselves. And yet, we suffer from impervious communication and from hellish solitude. This happens especially when we discover the inevitability of decline, not our own only but that of people and the world: nothing, no one, can escape decline; absolutely, we cannot save ourselves from the trap of aging and inevitable decline, from the journey to nothingness . . . Our only consolation remains deadly rhetoric!"

He did not say to her: "Our relationships lack something we cannot obtain, namely, to tell the truth always as it is and with no embellishment. If we could do that, we might have a seeming hope of finding that things were not what they were. But we cannot do that or rather we no longer can."

He said to her: "What is the purpose of life? What does it mean to you?"

She said: "I've never posed this question to myself. My life was defined by inner forces, by the influence of others, especially my family. Then there was also the foreigners' model of life during Tangier's international period . . . Since the time I entered school, I imitated my Spanish friends. There were exciting, attractive things and there was my own experience with you, don't forget that, artist. A large measure of coincidence directs us, but experience too brings us nearer to an understanding of the logic of things. My mother pursued me always with her experience and she kept insisting that I should get married. The experience of love uncovered many things but I did not want it to turn into a commonplace relationship. I felt that unknown worlds were waiting to be discovered and I did not ask what was the purpose of all that. After I got married and moved to Fez, I felt that I had taken the wrong path and that I would not be able to live within a cage. My reactions obeyed something organic within me, something I trusted but could not understand. Now I can tell you that the changes I experienced in my life were also influenced by the transformation of people and the world around me and by coincidence as well. I began to understand the importance of money and social rank, and I wanted to exploit my beauty to enter that kind of life, but I did not want to become a professional prostitute. I had a different image of my migration to Spain, but the pimp's scheme came to change everything and I was unable to withdraw after discovering his ruse. But life is always stronger than us and I entertained certain illusions, foremost of which was recapturing some happiness. As I grew older, all my concern went to my daughter Fatima so that I might realize through her what I had missed. And here you can see, even my new integration in society does not fill even a part of my aspirations, because I am aware of the game and its rules and I understand well that social appearances of religiosity do not rise to the true essence of religion, which increases my doubts.

"I don't wish my journey to end without gaining something that is my own, something that will compensate for my disappointment here and now; but Fatima abandons me. Whom should I complain to? I know you will say she has her own justifying reasons . . ."

He did not say to her: "There's a question we don't ask in tragic sincerity until we begin to decline. Before that, we're moved by illusions: love, money, power, ideology . . . When we discover their mirage-like character, we'll have become prisoners to them. So we resort to justification and to philosophizing, and we let ourselves be led to preparing for our death through strange ironical means, namely, through preserving our image formed by the others who shared our illusions, then through facing the bitterness that pursues us as we realize that we are deceived without being able to specify what was responsible for our deception. I am not sure that my paintings have achieved my purpose in life or that they will benefit others in achieving theirs. I am not certain that my life would have been happier if I had realized, from the beginning, that my purpose was mere illusions and that I had to live without them . . ."

He did not say to her: "I remember Justine in *The Alexandria Quartet,* who tuned her life to the rhythms of the sea. She interiorized its ebb and flow. She made passionate whims her guide to love and she surrendered her body to the fire of sex. She tormented those who loved her and desired her. She transformed all rituals and values, and set up only one unique ritual: absolute lust and group sex, away from the bonds of social relations and conventions. Was it an image of fire or of light that inhabited her and drove the blood in her veins? What she sought was the impossible self-realization, while the others around her were ecstatically raptured by their impossible love for her! But the ticking clock of decline led her—what a miserable illusion—to a kibbutz so that she might give meaning to her life! And there she was, looking down on us, embarrassed and timeworn, with her rough hands and with her flabby body that looked as if it had never swayed at the blowing of the breeze! Is it right for us, Justine, to ask: What is the purpose of life? Or does life realize its own purposes through us that we continuously don't know?"

Suddenly, he felt he could no longer say anything to her or to himself. Silence reigned. Beautiful silence. A summer evening wrapped the city. The sea. Dim lights sneaked across the veranda. Ecstasy ran in his veins. A beautiful woman was next to him. An old love? A former mistress? Time stretched out: it seemed to be far, then it appeared to be near as scenes from memory swarmed him, overlapping and crowding one another. Did questions have a meaning any longer?

He said goodbye to her and lay again on the sofa of the veranda without turning the light on. He had a sweeping desire for those moments of silence to stretch out as though suspended outside time.

A nap. Scenes from another world dispelled his melancholy and his low spirits: There was a transparent plastic mask on his face, like those worn by divers; on his back was an oxygen tank; and on his feet were rubber flippers to help him swim for a long time deep under the surface of the sea . . . To his right was Ghaylana and to his left her daughter, Fatima, both wearing the same equipment, and they were all proceeding merrily toward the ocean, diving deeper and deeper at an amazing speed. The fish made way for them. Their motions recurred with regular rhythm as though to the tune of quick music and the floor of the sea was covered with moss, sponge, and colored weeds. Then they all stood still, dazzled in the glow of the suppressed light at the sight of the huge whale, the shark, and the tuna. They were not afraid. Al-'Ayshuni saw himself take the plastic mask off his face and gesture to his two companions to do likewise. He breathed in a natural way and walked as though he were on solid ground. A short while later, a middle-sized dolphin approached and spoke to them in classical Arabic, saying, "Our queen, Murjana, mistress of the sharks and the fish of all kinds in this ocean, welcomes you in her kingdom and considers you guests extraordinary, and we, her subjects, will attend to you."

Fatima said joyfully, "Khurdaf, our teacher, spoke truly when he used to tell us that dolphins were more eloquent than men, and we didn't believe him!"

Addressing himself to the dolphin, al-'Ayshuni said, "Tell your queen that we are extremely grateful. We intended to take life asylum in her kingdom but she has generously offered us her hospitality as guests. This is a favor we'll never forget and I hope she will consider us her subjects and servants, I mean myself, my sweetheart, and her daughter . . ."

The dolphin interrupted, "Rather you and your two sweethearts. We know everything about you and that's why the queen has granted you the right of being her guest. Our concern is that you live here, in a free way; that's what you were obliged to conceal on the land above."

"How wonderful," exclaimed al-'Ayshuni as he put his arms around Ghaylana and Fatima and kissed them alternately. "I'm unable to thank you enough, brother dolphin."

He then took them to a small grotto, having all been freed from all that distinguished them from fish and other sea animals. Ghaylana and Fatima laughed and were rapturous, and al-'Ayshuni was dividing his attention between both. This was what he always dreamed of, what he lived out in secret and in an interrupted way, but now could practice with spontaneity and happiness under the water in the protection of the fish. Ghaylana appeared to be as young as her daughter. They resembled each other and they differed. It was a difference of flavor, perhaps, that drew him to each with the same avidity and infatuation. He felt he was at the highest point of rapture because time had disappeared here, or rather it was unified. What he had experienced earlier had no importance. It was this moment that he would make the beginning of his life history. But then, what was the use of history? Yours was only the hour you were in . . .

Days passed quickly in the sea. Queen Murjana's hospitable reception of her guests was beyond description as the three surrendered to rapture and the discovery of sea mysteries. Every morning, a song rippled through the water, sung by a melodious choir of dolphins:

> Everlasting azure
> Constant motion
> Incessant mysteries
> There's no time for slumber.
> Clear skies melt in the water
> And life's pleasure is eternal.

However, Fatima could not endure this felicity of enjoying the pleasures of body and soul. She surprised them one day, saying she wanted to return to the land. Ghaylana looked at her in amazement and Fatima said, "How much longer should we remain here, buried under the water? What do you both hope to get from this residence here?"

Ghaylana said, "We've come here to protect ourselves from the wickedness of people, from their envy, from their falsehood. The hospitality of the sea renews one's youth. Look at my body: it has become a blooming rose, as it was when al-'Ayshuni painted me twenty years ago. Is that not so, artist?"

Al-'Ayshuni said, addressing himself to Fatima, "We live here an eternal life. Doesn't this interest you?"

Fatima said sharply, "I am still in the prime of youth and do not accept this veiled retirement that you both impose on me. I've not been given life so that I may store it away. In spite of all that surrounds us in this beautiful dream, I've begun to feel I'm choking. Life exists before and after me, and no one will ask me what I've done with it; I'm the one who'll ask myself, the one who'll create the illusion that ties me to it in order not to feel I am frozen, dead, while still considered among the living."

Ghaylana said, "On land, I was not lucky. Here, all I wished for has perfectly come to be: that we live together in harmony and joy, away from all control. It doesn't bother me that my daughter becomes the sweetheart of my lover in the law of the sea but I also prefer to preserve my youth in order to enjoy al-- 'Ayshuni's love . . ."

Fatima interrupted her, "This here is no life, no eternity. At any rate, I don't care to live in eternity."

Ghaylana continued, "I don't want you to be obliged to take up the profession of prostitution like me—although I consider it to be a profession like any other. I know that you will not be able to endure the humiliation of your body every day. That's why I ask you: How can you yearn for a society in which no one has any criteria to differentiate between prostitution and other ways of life?"

"I have no answer," replied Fatima. "But I've decided to return to the land. Please, thank Queen Murjana and her retinue on my behalf for their excellent hospitality."

These words said, she turned around and swam upward.

Al-'Ayshuni looked at Ghaylana to ask what she intended to do. She quickly said she wanted to stay next to him this time; she did not want to lose him, for the hell of love was preferable to the hell of prostitution. He thought for a while, then said, "But I'm not sure whether my despair will not create lethal boredom in me, even when we are in the region of eternity; for I will then rebel against the queen of the sharks and the ocean, and our fate will then be nothing but two tombs in the belly of the huge whale."

AFTER these words, al-'Ayshuni woke up in terror, his throat dry. He woke up with a lump in his throat as though he were bidding farewell to a part of himself, a part in which the human was blended with the inanimate. He ran his hand over his body as though he felt it was still covered with sea moss. For a moment, he no longer distinguished between the limits of himself stretching on the sofa and himself in the course of the dream. It occurred to him that his state was a wonderful image of death. He sat up and began looking across the veranda to the darkness of the vanishing night and the first glimpse of rosy dawn, and he suddenly thought things were born at such moments. He wondered: were they born between the dusk of evening and the darkness of night, or between darkness and forenoon? He looked at the canvas and imagined seeing nebular lines and shapes in inner motion as though searching for a point, for a sperm to spark genesis and control rhythm.

4

During Fatima's stay with me, I was perplexed about her: she had invaded my life as my sweetheart's daughter, she acted with attractive maturity and sensitivity, she gave me to taste various kinds of physical pleasures . . . then she refused to tell me about her life.

Her letter to me after she had left is what shed light on some aspects of that fugitive face of hers . . .

—*From al-'Ayshuni's papers*

MY DEAR AL-'AYSHUNI,

I can imagine your reproof of me for not being in touch with you for over one year after our meeting. I had promised to be in touch and to meet you again in order to tell you about myself after having listened to you for a long time. But I did not feel I had anything to say, or rather I estimated that the time for that had not come. You frequently repeated that you did not know of what voice you were the echo, while I considered myself—and still do—as a person without a voice and unable to borrow any echo. When I visited you, I was trying to understand part of my past, of my relationship with my mother, Ghaylana. I was also thinking of a way to continue living after I had dismissed the idea of surrendering to weeping and self-pity.

I am writing to you now from the town of Menton, situated on the Italian border east of Monaco. I have come here in the company of my husband, Matthias Pedal, to visit his widowed mother, Madame Chantal. Menton is a quiet town with many parks, its climate is mild and dry, and it has many famous restaurants. Day before yesterday, Matthias invited me to one of them, Le Gourmet Restaurant, where we had an assortment of pastries stuffed with lobster, langoustine, and salmon, then a plate of veal filet done in delicious sauce flavored with wild herbs . . . I will not go into details lest your mouth begin to water for unattainable dishes . . .

But I have begun where I should have ended. What I have said so far will appear to you to be vague or merely a piece of news to be added to your information, when you rather expected me to speak in detail about my life, which, as you noticed, was different from my mother's. Am I really different from her? Yet, as you did when telling me about your life, I will try, as I write, to remember stations of my life journey that will help me understand what I went through, impelled—as I imagined I was—by instinct and by complicated circumstances stronger than the illusion of freedom that, for a long time, I thought was directing my steps.

I am approaching thirty and all my illusions have dissipated, or that is what I imagine, for tepidity is the overwhelming character of my relations with people and things, except when I take the role of the infatuated sweetheart with Matthias. Other than that, the world appears to me to lack the attractive illusion that used to move me at the beginning of my life journey.

I don't think that the hard year I spent in France before meeting Matthias was alone what weakened my enthusiasm and calmed down my impulse, for it was there that I had my college experience, "my love story" (Oh, artist! How sweet love is when we experience it in innocence for the first time!), and the period of loafing and idleness after I graduated from the university. I hasten to correct what I said about my marriage and divorce, for they did not take place, they never took place, and I preferred to claim that my daughter Nada was the fruit of marriage so that my mother would not be grievously distressed. However, I lived the experience with a different mentality when my relationship with al-Dawoodi, my friend at college, became strong. I discovered another world in the multitudes of students coming from various towns and regions, whose hearts were full of deprivation and rancor, and who had nothing but words to personify utopian dreams that had hardly any relation to reality. That dreamy character in particular was what struck me and gradually led me out of the rosy picture of life painted by my tolerant father, who had spoiled me to excess, and embellished by my mother, Ghaylana, who, during her visits to us, carried precious presents from Spain. When she spoke with me, she used to appear to me to have absolute power to achieve all my desires in return for my being a diligent student excelling in my studies. She spent money and I did well academically because, as she explained to me later, she wanted to realize through me what she herself had not been able to do.

It is neither easy nor enjoyable to relate my life story to you. It is a process that is not without stupidity in the final analysis. That is why I prefer to proceed by mentioning some landmarks and details in order to capture (this is what I imagine) what is beyond history and events, although it is part of them . . . For an event, then, will take the character of a transformer, and we will feel that the experience we are living constitutes a transition from one situation to others that are open to innumerable experiences not comprehended by the familiar way of understanding.

I remember that morning following the night of the wonderful dream, during my residence with you in Tangier. I woke up before you and went to the balcony of the sitting room. Soft sunlight colored the ripples of the sea and seagulls sang as they spread their wings in harmonious ascending and descending movements. Perched on the scattered rocks, shadowy fishermen loomed at the end of the slope as they sought to tempt probable fish with their fishing rods . . . I put a record on the record player, Mozart's *Piano Concerto No. 23* (Adagio), and I surrendered myself to the ecstasy of the event. Through the dialogue between the piano and the violins, I gradually began to betake myself to scattered clearings in the midst of a densely green forest. I stood in each clearing and raised my head to be drenched by the rays of the sun penetrating the branches. When the musical mode changed to a stronger tonality, I found myself running with a jump, spreading my arms and going through the undergrowth and the intertwining shrubs: there was nothing to obstruct my way, for I had been transformed into a musical note in Mozart's concerto! Then the melody became increasingly slow and I heard nothing but my own pulse in my veins and I smelled the warm earth overwhelming my pores, and everything around me and within me intermingled and was transformed into another being that took off toward an exciting, virgin land. At that moment, a feeling of beautiful fragility was born in me through which one could become everything and exist in everything . . .

I experienced a similar feeling at the beginning of my relationship with al-Dawoodi.

The College of Arts at the University of Fez was abuzz with all kinds of voices: there were nations and tribes, dialogues and altercations, and sometimes battles in which blood was shed. The police were continuously present on the university campus and classes were interrupted by protest strikes. A variety of provoking speeches invaded all ears, irrespective of caution and neutrality on the part of students like me. It was sufficient for a student to stand on the classroom platform and recite into the microphone a few inciting verses of poetry, such as:

> O people, whose right to life they denied,
> Will you abide in the slaughterhouse
> To be slain like sheep?
> Will you continue to wait
> For a loaf of bread from tax collectors?

The lecture room would be transformed into roaring throats, shouting slogans, and acclamations. It was a wonderful collective hysteria, difficult to resist. And although I was cool-headed, my curiosity was aroused in the second year and I began to follow up speeches and competing analyses.

Al-Dawoodi attracted my attention one day when he argued with the professor of the history of philosophy regarding certain concepts of Emmanuel Kant. He raised his hand, asking permission to speak, and said:

"I think that the way you have presented Kant's philosophy makes it look so ideal it cannot be criticized. I believe that his dependence on certain concepts of reason and of absolute circumstances, which he considers to be criteria for judgment, needs to be criticized from an opposite viewpoint, I mean, by relying on actual life experience, which also contains irrationality, intuition, and a degree of communication with others. Philosophy cannot be considered a forum for lawmakers who think they have the means to define reality . . ."

The professor interrupted, "This is facile criticism, which wants to be free from the bonds of reason. Besides, you have not read all Kant's texts, and in their original language, to be able to criticize him."

Al-Dawoodi responded, "I have depended on what you taught us, and you are, I think, fully conversant with Kant's philosophy . . . However, the matter as I see it is not a matter of pure knowledge. Am I here having lessons in order to abolish what I feel and experience? Or am I here to acquire knowledge through a process of comparison and connecting what others have written with what I feel and think?"

The professor smiled and ended the discussion, saying, "I never knew you were a budding philosopher, although you are still in your second year. We will wait to read your writings to compare you with Kant . . ."

On leaving the lecture room, I approached al-Dawoodi and asked, "I didn't fully understand your objection, for the professor teaches us what is in the prescribed syllabus. As for criticism, it can be done at a later phase."

He said, "My remarks touch on the method of teaching. The professor depends on transferring information that, however much he tries, will remain incomplete. I don't want him to summarize for me what I can read in the sources. I want to learn how to think in a way that connects me with my life experience."

I said, "He doesn't prevent you from doing that after you understand the lesson . . ."

He sharply interrupted: "Thinking happens through dialogue. What you suggest is soliloquy, rumination of information. I'm here to know how my friends think, how they react to what they learn. Otherwise, I'm not in need of college. You know that, after graduating, we'll not find a job. Therefore, we should at least seize the opportunity to think of what matters to us."

We had reached the gate of the college and the conversation between al-Dawoodi and me was still continuing. He asked if I lived in the university students' quarter, so I told him I lived in the city. He suggested that he should accompany me and I did not object. After a while, he turned to me and said:

"How do you explain the fact that, all last year, I did not get acquainted with any female student studying with me in the same classroom? We come and we go, or else we discuss things in meetings without being acquainted with one another. I have to thank Emmanuel Kant, who has given me the opportunity to get acquainted with a beautiful classmate like you, who is interested in what her classmates say."

I blushed and lowered my eyes, concealing my embarrassment with a smile. He continued:

"Let's leave Kant aside. I'd like to ask you: Do you make a point every day of realizing one absolute value by which you represent the human being that you are? Every morning, I feel a suffocating burden that begins with how I relate to my father, to the torrent of words I hear on radio and television, and then in the lecture room . . . Words, all of them, that don't reach down to what occupies me. I don't think I'm an exception in this matter, am I?"

I said, "What you say is correct, but I think that we tend to magnify our problems."

He interrupted, sarcastically, "We don't even speak about them, how can you claim we magnify them. Have you ever spoken with another female student about your situation as a women living in a society whose women are crushed?"

"I'm not crushed, nor are you. We are at the university and we know what others don't."

"You and I are crushed. Our diplomas are worth nothing. And you're more crushed than I am because you're a woman. Even if you were fortunate, in the eyes of society you belong to the tribe of women."

"This is philosophy . . ."

"Yes, I want it to be a philosophy that calls a spade a spade and speaks of the conditions we experience: a university in pursuit of students as though they were mice, grants not worth a nickel, highfalutin words blotting out the facts, distortion in all domains, castration of citizens wholesale and in installments!"

He spoke with passion that soon moved me. I found that I opened my eyes to see many things I had avoided thinking about. Moments later, he smiled apologetically and said:

"I'm giving you a headache about things you know better than I do. I should rather say something to entertain you and praise your beauty. Help me to find the words that would rise to the level of your honey-colored eyes and the magic of your captivating smile . . . Are you from Fez?"

"Almost. My mother is from Tangier."

"Oh, now I understand the suppressed calls of the sea coming from your eyes and lips."

"I thought you were more serious than that, especially because you are a budding philosopher, as the professor said of you."

"Seriousness will not solve our problems, and it may be a

mere mask behind which we hide our faults and our desires. Besides, the joy of hearts does not hurt anyone."

The event of meeting him overwhelmed me and I wished the road would never come to an end. I proceeded to tell him about my family, about my divorced mother working in Madrid, about my father who treated me like a friend, about novels that added to my soul things I didn't find in what I studied at college . . . Before we parted, we agreed to meet next morning to go together to the university.

That night, I slept overcome by exhilaration and emotion. I felt I was at the threshold of my first love, which I always wished would be like this. I was previously the spoiled, beautiful girl among the young men of the family; but with al-Dawoodi, I felt what I had lacked: a man who would converse with me, listen to my opinions, flirt with me and desire me and complain to me, a man who would share with me his fears and his questions . . . With him, I was no longer that female designed for doing what was expected of her: to study, achieve academic success, then marry and procreate—to represent values mostly based on hypocrisy and pretense.

Al-Dawoodi asked me one day whether our relationship would be limited to flirting, touching, and furtive kisses in empty lanes. I thought for a while, then I said, "Do you have any plan to escalate the battle, as you would say when giving a speech to masses of students?"

He nodded affirmatively and I did likewise.

"Remember that we won't live our lives twice," al-Dawoodi would say. "What is postponed is lost—at least in the life of this world."

And in tune with these words, we proceeded to escalate the

battle: his words and the touches of his skillful hands as well as my burning and effervescent body impelled me toward freedom from imagined prohibitions, and toward the horizon of liberation and defiance opened by the speeches of students who refused to die slowly, to be buried in the prime of youth.

These words are not sufficient to represent the immediacy of the situation at that time, I mean, to represent what made me feel I was created for a time different from that of my parents and grandparents. That's why I depend on your imagination, artist, to capture the details. Nevertheless, I will tell you about a scene that is difficult to skip: In a middle-sized room resplendent with whitewash, I sat with two female friends from college on rugs with wool pile in which red, yellow, and orange colors mixed. We were watching four songstresses dancing, along with al-Dawoodi and two male students who had accompanied my two female friends. That was in the town of Tiflit, during the month of April if my memory does not fail me. Al-Dawoodi had invited me to accompany him because one of his friends suggested we should spend the evening in a party at the home of a songstress he knew. After the tray of mint tea was passed around and after welcoming remarks were addressed to the male and female "professors," the beer that we had carried with us began to circulate. The bodies of the songstresses began to sway in accord with the rhythm of the *ta'rija* as they repeated Berber songs. The expressions of their faces were frank as were the movements of their bodies and the winks of their laughing eyes calling us to participate. Our "men" soon responded to their call and to the contagion of their dance. Meanwhile, we remained secluded in the corner, following the scene with our eyes as though their spontaneity had created a reaction in us against what we considered to be impudence or profligacy. Their movements came close to being sexual signals and our men lined up in front of them and responded to the luring vibrations of their bodies. We tried to follow the rhythm by clapping but the contraction of our bodies was clear and we soon returned to the role of onlookers. I felt as though we were not present, as far as al-Dawoodi and his two male friends were concerned, for their eyes all but protruded from their sockets as they stared at the faces and bodies of the songstresses and as the electrifying rhythm penetrated their limbs. When the dancing stopped and everyone sat down to rest and have a drink, Raqiyya, one of the songstresses, turned to us and said in a serious tone, "Rejoice and have fun with us, girls. This time for fun is not a time for watching. She who has anything to say to her lover, let her say it. As our forefathers said: Don't let the time for fun pass you by, even if it costs the cutting off of your head!"

"Yes, you're right, Lalla Raqiyya. We brought them here so that they may have some training with you. But they're falling asleep."

In the second round of dancing, our bodily inhibition was gone. I stood up with my two female friends and took part in the fray. And it seemed we were successful, for songstress Raqiyya commented as she followed our vibrations, saying, "Are you really at the College of Arts or the 'college' of escapades and songs?"

I mention this scene to you because I felt the collapse of a certain distance that separated me physically from the women—the songstresses and also the prostitutes. It was a distance formed by a disgusting idea about impudence and profligacy and insolence, as well as about the vulgar body . . . But in that evening, I became acquainted with a different image of "real" women, present through their bodies, their senses, and their language that says it as it is. I may not be accurate in expressing myself, but that does not matter because I want to let you know that, for me, artificial barriers have collapsed and that a new state of exciting curiosity to learn about other aspects of life has begun. What I used to read began to work in my mind and my imagination in a different manner, by relating relationships and comparisons to the actual experience of life and by giving precedence to the vital things moving within us. It was as though all my invisible bonds were untied that night, and I became unruly and spoke with spontaneity and daring. I distributed kisses to the songstresses, to my two female friends and their male companions, and I embraced al-Dawoodi and whispered to him that I desired his body, all his body, not excluding a single organ of it.

Occasions for the close union of our two bodies became prolonged, especially on Sundays and holidays. I would not leave al-Dawoodi's apartment before evening, his odor having stuck to my nose and his kisses having penetrated all my pores. Most often, I would linger on, unable to leave bed; and as he gently slapped my bare bottom, he would be obliged to repeat his expression that made us burst out laughing:"Now that we have liberated the body, let us go out to liberate the people."

His meetings were almost endless because, in addition to his student responsibilities, he was a member of a prohibited political organization. We used to agree on the general problems that continually beset the country, but we did not agree on the details. In our private discussions, I used to be closer to him but I was not very comfortable with his public interventions before the masses of students, perhaps because my politicization was limited, for I used to proceed from what I saw in daily life and I expressed it in a language that was raw in al-Dawoodi's view. But our small differences used to melt in the flood of our impulsive love. I began to have my secrets and to form my own opinions about what was happening. In that period, I did not know the pale and evil nature of monotony. I even began to be petulant with my father, whose relationship with me was characterized by excessive spoiling and friendliness, and I made him listen to my political analyses and to my comments on happenings in the country. Whenever I happened to surprise him sitting alone, leaning his back on the wall, I glimpsed a smile on his lips and I said to him:

"You always laugh with your angels."

His smile broadened as he said, "With my angels and with the specter of my gazelle-like daughter."

I altered my tone and said, "Listen, dear father. I would like to discuss with you the problems that are happening."

"Okay, what's happening now?"

"Don't you hear the news? The rising cost of living, the workers dismissed from their jobs, the strike at our college entering its fifth day . . ."

"Yes, so what? It's not the end of the world. Why do you have to carry the whole world on your shoulders? Your condition hasn't pleased me lately. You should rather spend your time studying, as your mother wants. Keep away from this nonsense. It profits you nothing."

I did not surrender to his logic, and I went on analyzing the consequences of the policies followed and of the increasing impoverishment, and I told him what happened to some of our acquaintances, exaggerating sometimes and giving invented details at other times . . .

He listened calmly, then said, "Permanence in any situation is impossible, praise to Him who is ever-abiding and eternal. As for you, I don't want you to be upset. One of your laughs is worth millions to me."

How much are sweet words worth? Kind words that accumulate in our depths to give us glow and the desire to live when days and nights become dark in our eyes, making us walk as though in clouds of haze? My father's words were an antidote that dissipated my distress, an opportunity to calm down my extravagant ardor. But I was impelled to absorb all events and to experience their details as though I were one of the history makers of that period. I accustomed myself to discard my inherited habits, to be independent of the family cocoon, to go on personifying rebellion and following the dictates of my whims. Only now, when a long time separates me from the fever of adventure and rosy dreams, do I realize the deception of things and the mercurial quality of experience, and also the abiding existence of sweet words in my memory. I realize, I distinguish—but I do that with a neutrality whose coldness consumes the joy of the self and its spontaneous inclination to ecstasy. I now use the quality of neutrality to diagnose my present condition, although I am not confident that the result coincides with what my perception and my passion have turned out to be . . . Perhaps as I proceed to write this letter, I will find other qualities as well as other reasons, different from those I wrote earlier. But the thing I will not hesitate to consider as the beginning of my transformation from the ecstasy of assimilation to the weakness of defeat is al-Dawoodi's arrest.

My memory (How exhausted it is!) calls up the first moments when the news arrived, then it reviews my attendance at the trial, al-Dawoodi's daring and enthusiastic declarations, his look at me when he was sentenced to four years' imprisonment, and my visits to him in prison to supply him with books and lecture notes so that he could take the examination to obtain the *Licence* . . . I am not sure, but it seems to me that, at that time, I had an intuition that a crack in the course of my life was beginning to have its first fissure. A moist drop had settled in my womb a month before al-Dawoodi was arrested, and I did not want to tell him lest he should ask me to abort it. Thinking of it now, I imagine I was eager to experience my liberation to the full, but I do not regard it as unlikely that, by keeping the fetus, I intended to bring around my sweetheart al-Dawoodi to marriage. Only in the fourth month did I inform him about the life being formed in my womb. He looked at me through the prison bars, astonished at first, then he smiled and nodded his head, trying to find words to express his joy. Perhaps he understood I was clinging to my pregnancy and so he blessed my choice.

I don't want to neglect a detail that happened on the same day I visited him and told him about the fetus. When I left the prison, I was suddenly overwhelmed by a feeling of loneliness and of being unjustly treated. I found that I was facing the world, for the first time, with my freedom, which was beginning to bind my movements. With foggy but wingèd perception, I felt the difficulty of my lonely passage through the maze of experiencing, on my own, the failure of hopes and the collapse of illusions. Suddenly tears began to flow from my eyes, so I said in stubborn disregard, "These tears are without crying, they're mere tears." But I soon began to sob and to weep audibly. I stopped under a tree and surrendered to wailing, not heeding those around me. I became aware of a man's voice, kindly asking what had befallen me. He offered to take me in his car and I did not object. He was a good listener, so I told him all about my situation. He sympathized with me and told me he too passed through such an experience when he was a student. He invited me to have a drink and to listen to music, so I accepted his invitation. The meeting turned into moments of real tenderness that softened my grief and my loneliness. I knew I would not meet him again, but the atmosphere that his kind words and treatment created as well as my need for quenching my accumulating thirst made me live out that transient adventure with burning surrender. When we parted, he gave me an amount of money and asked me to buy some books for my imprisoned friend and to tell him that, out there, there were those who thought of him and his friends, and who appreciated their courage, etc. . . . As I was returning home, pressing the money in my hand, a spell of hysterical laughter took hold of me: I found myself in a situation I had not intended. I was responding to an inner need for communication, but the incident ended with a cheap consolation by which the man wanted to ease his feeling of guilt and, in turn, I sensed the gratuitous nature of what I had done. Al-Dawoodi's words and his features filled me and put my blood on fire, yet I went and slept with a stranger. Was it my fear of walking alone on a rough road that was taking me from the abstractness of encounter to its real potholes and stumbling blocks? In the fit of hysterical laughter, accompanied by tears of feeling how unjust and absurd life was, I decided to tell my father the truth about my relationship with al-Dawoodi so that he would help me bear the burdens of my choice. He said that what I had done would anger my mother, Ghaylana, and she would accuse him of collusion with me. That's why he suggested that I should claim I had married al-Dawoodi secretly before his arrest. He further advised that, before anything else, I should study hard in the remaining months before the examination of the *Licence* and pass so that we could control some of my mother's wrath. I agreed with him regarding what he requested, but I was determined to confront Ghaylana when she came to visit us in the summer of that year. I had my doubts about the nature of her work and I was getting fed up with her oblique, insincere words with me. It was as if she did not perceive my transformations; she saw them but did not take them into consideration, beginning with the maturing of my body and the change in my language. She always used her intelligence to make me believe that things were going as she had planned them and that I was still a constant element in the picture she had drawn as she wished. In my view, she was no longer that mother who charmed others with her elegance, her language, and her strong personality, because in her inadvertence I had enlarged my circle of experience and of seeing and understanding things.

As I expected, the examination results were positive as far as al-Dawoodi and I were concerned. Meanwhile, my belly was growing increasingly but I succeeded in concealing my pregnancy from my friends at college. Al-Dawoodi advised me to stop attending public gatherings to protect the fetus.

I visited him behind bars, but I felt he was increasingly absent despite his abundant presence in my womb. I had a sensation of emptiness. The fullness I had experienced next to him when I began my adventure of love and defiance receded. I was weak and spent many mornings lying down, running my hand over my belly and recalling the moments of being united with al-Dawoodi in love. My father persisted in caring for me and in overwhelming me with his tenderness and encouragement. But the pain of absence drew me to al-Dawoodi and secretly dug its furrows in my soul. My suspicions were aroused. I no longer found in our conversations across the prison bars any support for my passionate emotion. I reinterpreted every word al-Dawoodi uttered during my visits and found in each word evidence of his flagging love or of his annoyance with this expected baby I had imposed on him.

Two months after Nada was born, my mother came to Fez for her annual visit. It was an early evening in November, as I recall, and some slight rain was falling in the courtyard. I was in the kitchen preparing supper and my father was tenderly talking to Nada in the central room. Some time passed before my mother could understand what she was seeing. My father jokingly said to her that we had found Nada one morning in swaddling clothes in our courtyard and that I had chosen a name for her and decided to adopt her . . . But Ghaylana looked at me with examining eyes and repeated her questions. My father took her by the hand and asked her to come upstairs with him so that he could explain everything to her. She remained calm, or rather pretended to be calm, until I later heard her scream in rage:

"God bless you, Buster! You let her marry without telling me! And to whom? To one imprisoned for political reasons, one who will make her lose her future . . ."

I ran upstairs and held my father by his hand, begging him to leave both of us alone because I wanted to reveal everything to her. She tried to attack me but I pushed her hands violently away from me, fixing her face with fierce eyes as though I were aware for the first time that I was no longer the spoiled child she thought I was. Words poured out of my mouth with speed and succession as though they were shot from a handgun. I emphasized to her that I was free to get married, to prostitute myself with anyone I liked and at any time I wanted, and that she could not enslave me with her money which I knew now how she earned . . . I saw her face flush and her body tremble, but she soon took hold of herself and burst out in a nervous, sarcastic laugh:

"Good for you, professor! Now you've got the news that your mother prostitutes herself in order to provide for you and educate you . . . And what's wrong with that? I do not steal. I live by the sweat of my brow but it is my money that you waste . . ."

Dialogue between us was in earnest; I mean, confrontation became real. For I found my mother Ghaylana to be more intelligent than I had imagined. She began to bare her soul and reveal her past frankly in a manner that made me feel insignificant. All that I had experienced in life, which, in my estimation at the time, was exciting and agitating, seemed trivial to me, childish when compared to what she was relating and using as argument.

I don't want to repeat what you know, because you related it to me yourself when I visited you at home. But I will tell you that she spoke of you with admiration and sowed in me the seeds of jealousy at the time, so I decided to snatch you from her. Once more, I realize my thoughtlessness.

"No man and no woman can save one another," she would say with agony. "Each is hung like a sheep from its trotter. This is what I have always wanted to make you understand in light of my life experience. And I waited until you would complete your university education to reveal to you what experiences I had in store for you. I don't want you to walk, as I did, on a winding dark road. You can experience love in a thousand ways without letting it transform you into confetti blown by the wind . . ."

What confetti and what wind, mother Ghaylana? Who is

protecting whom? Yes, I am your daughter. But it is my right to live my own life, to experience it with all its surprises and tragedies. I have hated guardianship and censorship and the role of being a meek doll. However strong your logic is, it does not persuade me . . .

She spoke and I spoke. I did not show any weakness in facing her because the warmth of my adventure was still filling me and because my way appeared to me, up to that time, as leading to the realization of some of the dreams al-Dawoodi and I had cherished. The dialogue was lengthy and punctuated by tears and sobs and then by kisses. My father came upstairs to urge us to come downstairs and have supper.

At that moment she turned to me and said, "I'm telling you in front of your father that I bought a villa in Tangier this week, and that you may live in it if you so wish until I finally return from Madrid. If you desire to go abroad to continue your studies, I am prepared to cover your expenses as I promised you when you were in your first year at the university. I have endured what I did only for your sake . . ."

Waiting: that is what I have come to live on. I wait for al-Dawoodi to get out of prison, I wait while looking for a job, I wait for Nada to say her first words and to walk her first steps so that movement and chaos may come to our quiet home. Before leaving, my mother Ghaylana gave me the key to the villa and told me its address, and she reminded me that my grandmother could keep me company when I went to Tangier.

If I were to use my language now and not the language of that period, if I were to tell you about my psychological contrition after Nada's birth and my confrontation with my mother and my surrender to waiting, I would say that I was being depleted every day and that emptiness was growing within me and rising to fill my soul, to absorb my curiosity and replace it with indifference. This change stole into me from the outside too, from things and words and scenes I picked up in moments of boredom and distress.

As I sat on a bench in a public park with Nada, a veiled old woman asked me why I was so sad when my daughter was as beautiful as the moon. I told her that I was thinking of her father who was far away from us. She asked about the reason for his being away and I said:

"He works in France and it is a year since we saw him last."

"Poor woman," she said. "Be patient. Working abroad is fine, for there are no more jobs here. And anyone who does find a job is made to work like a slave."

I thought I could take any role that other women took. What frightened me more was the invisible, overwhelming power of what we call society with its appearances and its classifications, in which contradictory values mix, sometimes appearing to be equal and equitable so that we cannot distinguish between them. I remembered Kant and al-Dawoodi's discussion with the philosophy professor, I remembered the books and articles I read, and I smiled: What a difference between this and that. I am alone now, Nada is in my lap or next to me, my father continues to be caring and spends his time between worship and musical entertainment, my mother Ghaylana sells her body and showers me with her money, al-Dawoodi in the midst of four walls is—I feel—slipping away from me, and my rebellion has lost its effectiveness . . . The cracks are getting wider but I can't pinpoint their cause and I am unable to transcend them.

How can I resume the life of expectation? I face this question

every morning. I tried to occupy myself with reading books and
newspapers but my boredom and my anxiety continued. I suggested to my father that I should go to Tangier for a while to
change scenery and visit my grandmother there.

In Tangier, I was able to be reconciled to myself. I got acquainted with some young women at the café and I invited them
to dinner at the villa. I was attracted toward that strange world of
theirs, which appeared to me to be enigmatic while I was in my
state of confusion. They were young women with a strong
physique, overflowing with youthfulness; they wore elegant
dresses and costumes; they smoked and laughed noisily. Some of
them worked at lawyers' offices, or at hospitals and bars. Some of
them introduced themselves as "unemployed women living in
luxury and looking for a job." I thrust myself among them every
evening and I entertained myself by listening to them. We were
sometimes joined by youths and men who knew them. To me,
relations were open and characterized by exciting spontaneity:
they spoke about everything, they were frank with one another,
they criticized one another, they variously acted the roles of free
young women in love and wives left waiting at home. On my
part, I refused the advances made by some of those who frequented the café. Those young women often took it upon themselves to protect me from the inducements. After the gratuitous
adventure I had in Fez, I came to live with some kind of regret
and I was determined to keep myself for al-Dawoodi, who was
nestled in the cells and pores of my body.

In the company of that new circle, I found an entertaining
pleasure. I gradually regained my ability to compare, to observe,
to communicate. They were women with a different language
and with daring behavior, and theirs were not the familiar values.

They were united by a love for life devoid of philosophizing. They knew the secrets of the notables of Tangier as well as of those who had arrived recently, and they joked about some of the scenes they witnessed or heard of, meanwhile retaining a kind of intimate collusion that created what resembled an alliance among them. I was enchanted to look at any two young women of them telling each other their secret worries: I noticed their understanding looks, their sorrowful facial features, their mutual hand squeezing, their eyes bathed in tears, and their comforting smiles . . . Hardly anything existed outside the two young women confiding in each other. I spent several days before I got rid of my cerebral reactions in dealing with them; then I learned how to speak spontaneously, to laugh without restraint, and to exchange kindnesses tenderly. From time to time, I wrote to al-Dawoodi about my experiences in Tangier and about my discovery of that group of young women. I limited myself to descriptions of scenes of our sessions, for I had not yet formed an opinion about them but was somewhat enchanted by that behavior that gave a woman's world a live existence compared to the traditional world which I rejected during my rebellion at college. Outside the criteria of shame, of correct and forbidden behavior, those women dwelled in the fabric of society in different situations but they spoke and struggled skillfully within the rules of the game.

My association with them restored the attraction of my mother's story: it was like the drivel of a novelist jotted down before it was actually realized. What was I to her and to them? A philosophizing intellectual who was bringing up her daughter and waiting for her sweetheart to marry her upon his release from prison. What if he changed his mind? What if we did not find a job? Would we get married and live as a burden on my mother or his father? What a narrow horizon! How short was the path that this love was leading us on! I ended my contemplations with such dramatic statements.

I was alone in Fez with Nada, at noontime, talking tenderly to her after she woke up. The cooing of pigeons was heard coming from the roof and the noises of the neighboring houses rose and died down without being intelligible to me. What raged confusingly in my mind and in my imagination was not intelligible to me either, for I was still strongly drawn to the experiences I had in Tangier and, from time to time, remembered al-Dawoodi's forthcoming release from prison in six months. Everything seemed near and distant. Events lost their sharpness and it was as though I were executing a plan drawn in my absence. From waiting to waiting, from one atmosphere to another—my memory was like a recording machine in which the tapes overlapped one another. I sometimes tried to put all that my memory had stored on one single page in order to see it all at once and to comprehend the experiences I had and what was lying ahead for me.

But the image disappeared because the page was soon blurred like water in which a stone was thrown. After the examination and after giving birth, I kept away from college and my friends. I had no job and al-Dawoodi was the only expected horizon for me, although I did not know how we would behave after his release. He did not broach the subject during my visits to him and I did not want to preoccupy him with this concern . . . I heard the sunset call to prayer and expected my father would soon return home. I put Nada in her carriage and pushed her to the kitchen so that she would be next to me as I prepared supper. Moments later, my father's joyful voice reached me:

"Good evening. And may the bride and her daughter be blessed. What's the news?"

"The news is with you," I said. "I've been at home all day."

"And the newspapers, don't you read them anymore?"

"I've not touched them for a week."

"No, no. This is unbelievable. How else could one have specially pleasant news."

I looked at him to ask but he quickly said, "Happy Si al-Dawoodi, he's out of prison for three days now, he and a few of his friends. It's a royal pardon and all the people at the café are talking about this."

I was stunned and did not utter a word. My father came close to me to embrace me and congratulate me; then he bent over Nada and picked her up in his arms to dandle her and play with her.

I did not know al-Dawoodi's address in Casablanca. And I could not understand what had happened other than what was generally published in the newspapers . . . I went back to waiting, surprised at how he did not get in touch with me as soon as he was released from prison, for he knew my address. A week later, I received a letter from him that I prefer to copy for you because it dispenses with any comment by me:

Dear Fatima,

You have, no doubt, heard about my release from prison with some other friends, by virtue of a royal pardon, before the completion of our sentence. I found that my family was present to greet me and so I could not get in touch with you. At any rate, I found that my father was intent on making me aware of the necessity of abandoning political activity in order to catch up with what I had missed. On the very first day, he said to me that he had informed certain responsible officials that he would "guarantee" my behavior after prison. That's why he offered me the job of being in charge of administering his project of hatching turkeys, now experiencing an increasing expansion in the market. Many things had quickly changed in our society and, when I analyze the experiences we had, I find that I was reckless and that idealism was what made me think I could act on behalf of others to change conditions. What was the result? I told you about the climate of the feverish debates and of the reciprocated accusations I experienced in prison with my friends, and you know the harshness of the isolation I suffered last year. True, there was your love, our romantic experience . . . But I was struck by fear whenever I thought of the closed doors that would await us after prison. That's why I accepted my father's offer in order to put an end to my misery and vagrancy, and perhaps to being imprisoned again.

In his conversation, my father is bent on making me realize that he is planning for my future and that he places specific conditions on this matter, which I have to respect. That's why I can't now inform him of our planned marriage or of Nada's birth before concluding the marriage. This is a problem for which we will later think of a suitable solution.

This position of mine may be shocking to you but I hope you will understand the circumstances that imposed on me this kind of temporary yielding which, I hope, will be in the interest of both of us. I assure you that I am ready to help you financially until you find a suitable job and until I am able to organize my affairs and regain my father's trust. Other than that, I can't promise anything because matters seem to be unclear and confused, and I need time to comprehend what has happened and is still happening.

I kiss you and Nada, and hope to visit you both soon.

Al-Dawoodi

If I were well-versed in the craft of novelists and storytellers, I would have stopped here for a moment to describe to you "the state of shock" I was in on reading al-Dawoodi's letter, and to represent to you my deep sorrow, my renunciation of the world, my thinking of suicide because I was facing the collapse of a great hope for the first time. But, as I write to you to inform you and to relieve myself, and perhaps to understand what I myself went through up to now, I only convey to you what I felt at that time without any retouching.

I don't deny that I felt as though someone had given me a violent blow when I finished reading the letter, and then I felt something like a shiver after a cold shower in the depth of winter. But I moved to another state in the same day and felt as though I were living an experience I had expected earlier during my waiting for the release of al-Dawoodi from prison. It even seems to me now that my position as a beloved woman and as a suspended wife of an imprisoned fighter had been transformed within me secretly and made me drawn—in moments of solitude and mental rumination—to an open condition, to an unprecedented experience that had no clear horizon, yet a condition that took me out of the state of waiting and lassitude.

Was my mother's experience haunting me and attracting me? Or was it her pride that woke up in my depths when I decided to resort to defiance? The philosophy I studied, the books I read, and the dreams I stored up would not prevent me from lying naked in life's uncharted sea. I began to tell myself that it was al-Dawoodi's right to change directions (for the mind that did not move was a disaster) and to bet on hatching cocks and hens to realize his father's dream: "looking forward to producing hens, each of which would weigh seven kilograms as was the case in Austria." When al-Dawoodi used to relate to me such statements of his father's conversations, he did not fail to mock his father's narrow commercial mentality for he wanted to change the world, rebel son that he was. He has only now discovered that Kant, Hegel, and Marx will not lead to anything but isolation in prison and life on the margin . . . It is his right then to return to the cackles of turkeys; perhaps they will be clearer to him than the obscurities of philosophy. Haven't we learned to respect another person's opinion and choice, regardless of differences between us? It would be useless for me to ask him to fulfill the promises that we whispered to each other at the height of ecstasy and union of our two bodies. What got hold of me more than anything else was that, as I said to you earlier, I was beginning to move to another region that seemed more open in my imagination, in spite of the fact that I also guessed its suffering.

Perhaps that same night, I calmly made a decision: I will not live on the income of anyone and I will never be a burden on al-Dawoodi, who is preoccupied with insuring a stable future under the wing of a turkey project and the satisfaction of a respectable family. My daughter Nada will live with her grandfather, by the sweat of my mother Ghaylana's brow. As for me, I will have to leave this happy kingdom like hundreds of other men and women.

When I visited you in Tangier that evening (more than a year and a half ago?), I did that out of curiosity, for I wanted to draw a full picture in my mind of my mother by getting acquainted with the lover of her youth, especially because she had spoken of you at length after our encounter, of which I gave you an account in this letter. Before that, Ghaylana's image in my mind coincided with that of a woman who was created fully mature, who knew all the mysteries of life, and who could not be taken away from her seriousness or her plan by any emotion or event. I found her beautiful and did not imagine her as a lover. I used to ask my father about her and the poor man used to sigh, then mutter, "May we not fall in love with a stone." Yet when she spoke of her love story with you, she regained her lost glow and was overwhelmed by an equivocal fragility . . . Furthermore, I was obliged to stay in Tangier in order to obtain a passport, so I said to myself that that was a good opportunity to have a complete history of my family and get acquainted with a painter living on the margin, whose memory stored up fragments from the album of international Tangier and its language. I used to like what my mother told me about the city and about its people in that golden period, and so I found that I was attracted to the nostalgia of past days which I had not experienced.

"This isn't Tangier," Ghaylana used to say. "Tangier went away with its people."

In your words and the way you spoke, I found the nostalgia that had taken hold of my imagination, so I stayed with you as long as I could, and I enjoyed it. But I was convinced of the necessity of leaving Morocco in order to search for another experience, perhaps because of what you told me in detail about my mother.

To continue my studies did not occur to me, although I mentioned that as a pretext when applying for a passport. And this was not sufficient as you know, for I had to pay another price, which I did without hesitation because I was ready to do anything for the sake of leaving the country. While in Tangier that month, I considered myself free from anything I used to be earlier. I often repeated, "Even prostitution in Europe will be better than it is here . . . At least I will earn more!" As for my adventure with you, I considered it a farewell to that other "I" which I inhabited in the period of love illusions and of aspirations to a more beautiful life. You appeared to me to be from another planet and in agreement with a concept of life I now find to be mythical.

When I recall you, I remember your facial features dominated by perplexity as you muttered, "I don't know to which voice I am the echo." And I remember asking myself: Is it reasonable that an educated painter like you can lose his voice to become a mere echo to an unknown source? This statement, no doubt, was made by a poet or a writer and it stuck in your mind, so you hid behind it in order to preserve your innocence. It is not important for me now to tell you that, because I always admired your ability to live events and to speak about them, distancing them from yourself as if they were a shadow of a life and not your own life itself.

After arriving in Paris, I spent the first month totally given up to my soul's desires and instincts. I lived in a small hotel in the Eleventh Arrondissement and I set aside an amount of money I brought with me from Morocco to live for a few weeks like a tourist in this city about which I had heard and read a lot. I went out in the morning and came back only at midnight or later. I toured the historical sites and visited the museums, but I allotted more time to wandering in the streets and alleys looking at faces, listening to people's speech, and loafing about on the banks of the Seine River. I ate a sandwich or a piece of pastry most of the time, and I continued walking and roaming about, the cinema being one of the stations of my daily trip. I was like a blank page that wanted to be filled with what it saw and heard, and I learned to respond spontaneously to the offers of others: to the flirtations of men, to the comments of madmen and vagabonds, to the conversations of male and female tourists. I felt tremendously happy all that month, perhaps because I avoided thinking of putting my situation in order and securing my residence in France . . . and why don't I say also because that kind of touristic life helped me to forget what I had experienced earlier? It was a fascinating life and its taste is still in my mouth, as we say. It yielded bright memories, from which I seek help in hours of melancholy and boredom: conversations I had with old women in the Luxembourg Garden about their lives and children, transient meetings I had that might end with sex and exchange of addresses with tourists who—I knew—would never write to me or whose letters I would never answer . . . What is important is that every morning of that month I used to feel I was light, fresh, passionately fond of all I would come across that day.

I remember this first relationship of mine with Paris because it helped me inwardly to accept emigration, making it for me a natural horizon dissolving all that preceded it. Shall I say that the atmosphere of Paris hid behind this transformation? In Paris, despite its expanse, its plenitude, and its abundance of places to meet people, I felt for the first time that I carried my freedom on my shoulder and that its weight was heavy, suffocating, impossible for me to get rid of. Nobody would help you with your freedom, and if you could not shoulder its burden, there was no place for you in the atmosphere of the city. This was a feeling I had never experienced in Fez or Tangier: their atmosphere remained blended with friendly sociability and mercy, and so you would be under the delusion that others were ready to carry your burden of freedom for you.

After the month of rest that I gave myself, I began to deal with practical matters. I registered myself in graduate studies and established relationships with male and female students; I began to look for a secret job, and I tried several. But I will stop at one experience because it made me change my behavior. I had come to know a Philippine woman who worked at the home of a French bourgeois family. When I told her of my circumstances, she offered to help me find a job with a rich family from the Arabian Gulf. The husband was approaching sixty and his wife was over forty, her face not resisting signs of early old age. They had a son studying in London and about to be married in the summer holidays. Everything went on in a usual manner in the months before the wedding. But when we moved to the Riviera, near Nice, for the final arrangements of the wedding, my troubles began with the old man from the Gulf. He began to follow me with looks that sought the details of my body and he started calling me Miss Fatima instead of My Daughter Fatima. I immediately realized that my youth had excited his lust. On the wedding night, we went to Les Corsaires Restaurant to have dinner with members of the bride's and the groom's families and their friends. At the beginning, we were given a large number of empty plates and were guided to stairs in the middle of the garden; we climbed the stairs to the top, then each one began to break the plates in quick movements as he or she descended on the other side of the stairs. We all jumped like monkeys, causing uncouth noise that was contagious. At first, I hesitated to take part but some guests pulled me by my hand and made me join the game: dozens of plates broken, loud music, jumping on the stairs, holding each other by the waist innocently and intentionally, and glasses of alcoholic drinks flowing . . . Hardly would the din subside for a moment when the bridegroom would get up and run to the plates in order to break them with evident pleasure and ask his friends to follow suit. Then Arab dancing began and the old man from the Gulf came to urge and propel me to the dance floor. My body gradually shed the maid's gravity that I had forced upon it and my eloquent movements attracted the attention of certain dancers. They swayed harmoniously with the spiral motions of my hips and buttocks. All of a sudden, the father pulled himself up to me and, with a smile on his face, he whispered, "I ransom you with my soul, O gazelle of the Atlas." I continued dancing, searching with my eyes for his wife, and I saw her watching us with grim looks. I stopped dancing but he pulled me by my hand and I was unable to resist. My senses had begun to be numb with recklessness and release, especially after I had drunk enough champagne to be on fire. I don't remember the remaining details of the evening party, which went on till dawn. I only remember that the fragments of broken plates filled the garden of the restaurant and that we could no longer dance except with difficulty. Many men and women fell on the floor, laughing and inebriated, and the waiters rushed to help them. Did anyone carry me, in a state of intoxication, to one of the hotel rooms? Did anyone's hand steal into the area under my navel? I can't be sure of anything. But I woke up at about noon the next day, shaken vigorously by the hand of the man's wife. She told me that they would be leaving for Italy with their son and his bride and that she was dispensing with my services and offering me a generous compensation so that I could return to Paris and look for another job.

She was rude and curt. I remembered her grim looks as I danced with her husband the day before. I did not object, was there any use?

I returned to my little room at the Voyage Hotel in the Eleventh Arrondissement. The hotel owner welcomed me and asked whether I was on a transient visit. I explained to him that I wanted to stay for a few months. My pocketbook full of the gift of the old man's wife had encouraged me to say that. But my mind was really distracted and I could hardly know my inner state of being. "Empty of all feeling" may be the nearest expression for that vagueness that enwrapped me after I boarded the train from Nice to Paris. It was as if the five days on the Riviera with their luxury and din, their banquets, their plate-breaking party, and their dancing 'till dawn had evaporated from my memory or had become so distant as to belong to some ancient time. A veil stretched before my eyes, making all that I saw or all that my imagination conjured up appear clouded and faded. Why do I dwell on these details while I narrate to you this experience? Because, as I came down the steps at the Lyon train station in Paris, I felt that there was nothing connecting me with anything: neither times and their divisions, nor persons and what we normally call values. I felt I could do and accept everything with the same neutrality or neutral enthusiasm, not caring to move from one thing to its opposite. If I had been held and violently shaken by two strong hands, I would have had no reaction and my vacant look would not have changed. I no longer belonged to anything and it gave me no pain to know I had come to be so. When I now recall all that was crammed into my brain about identity, history, and the homeland, I find that that effort and all those words are not worth anything when compared to that state which took

hold of me and emptied me of all charges of memory and con-
nections with the past. Only one thing guided me now: the instinct to continue living in Paris in any manner and at any price.
I did not want to belong to anything here because I did not care
to compensate for what I had lost. I wanted to live at the zero
point, one day at a time, without expectations or delusions. Do
you remember what you used to tell me about your suffering as
you pursued features of paintings looming in your imagination
without giving you their secrets? Perhaps through my verbal de-
piction of the state I endured, you can paint a portrait of an emptied, suspended woman who was beyond words and beyond
embellished past memories. I think that painting helps more than
words.

After several days of seclusion in the hotel, I felt a desire for
going out and loafing about in the streets of Paris, as I had done
on my arrival. This time, I had no delusions of getting a job or
making an effort to attend classes in order to specialize in modern philosophy, which I found to consist of riddles beyond my
understanding. I wandered about, occupying myself with everything my eyes fell upon: faces looking out of buses or persons re-
laxing on chairs of cafés; dresses, suits, overcoats, and blouses in
shop windows; newsstands; bookstores; buildings redolent of ancient and modern history at every turn; Gothic and baroque
churches whose domes and filigreed columns rose to heaven; and
bumper-to-bumper cars in slow parallel lines in the rush hours—
and how many there were! But all that no longer aroused my curiosity. I was searching for the most trivial things and scenes in
order to make them a topic of thought that would occupy me
and take possession of my mind. For a whole week, I found myself occupied with the topic of dog-do strewing the sidewalks,

both in the wealthy neighborhoods and in the less wealthy residential areas. What added to my interest in the topic of dog-do was that I had heard a program on the France Inter radio devoted wholly to this problem, which annoyed those who did not own dogs and which disgusted tourists. I remember that one of the panelists made a suggestion that the mayor of Paris should announce a generous award for anyone who could protect the City of Light from the excrement of dogs. I said to myself: Why don't I try my luck? For I might invent a means that would permit me to win the award, and perhaps a permanent post in the municipal administration of Paris. I spent several days observing those who took their dogs for a walk in the streets. I walked behind them to capture the smallest details of the places the dogs chose to urinate or defecate. I sometimes approached the dog's owner and tried to start a fake conversation about the beautiful animal. I asked about its pedigree, its qualities, and its habits before I reached the subject of urination and defecation. When I asked the dog owners about their attitude to finding a means to protect the city from the filth of those tame animals, they smiled and said they did not have any objections, provided the freedom of the dogs was not curtailed!

I busied myself with drawing two figures, one of which was circular and the other cylindrical, to represent rubber devices tied with thread to a dog, the former device to its rear and the latter to its lower belly. I was happy about what I designed and surprised that no one before me had thought of such a solution, and I said that coincidence was often behind inventions. I took my project to the municipality of Paris and asked to be received by the person in charge of the city's cleanliness. After a short wait, I was invited to the office of a lady who was over fifty years old and who had a triangular face with sharp features. Her dark blue clothes granted her an air of dignity and severity. She gave me a half-hearted smile as she motioned me to a seat. She asked about the reason for my visit and I explained the idea to her by referring to the radio program I had heard, and I handed her my project, which I had labelled "Let us help our dogs to be more discrete." She examined the papers with the drawings and the explanation, then she said, "This is ingenious, Mademoiselle. It's a wonderful idea and I'll present it to those responsible and hope it will meet with their approval."

I gave her my address and left her office, elated. I decided to continue looking out for opportunities like this one that would perhaps open for me possibilities of trying my inventiveness, which I had just discovered thanks to the dogs of Paris. My joy did not last long, for I received a letter from the municipal department of cleanliness thanking me for my initiative and informing me that a similar project had been submitted in 1961 by a French citizen named Rounart Bichon, that it had been presented to dog owners, and that they had protested and objected to it because it would add to them the chores of emptying the diapers of the dogs, cleaning them, and breathing bad smells that would make them hate their tame animals. This made the municipality of Paris reject the proposal. The letter of the person in charge closed with an apology because she had not known about that former project; meanwhile she referred me to the municipal archives if I wanted to learn about Rounart Bichon's project, which differed from mine in some technical details.

During that critical period, I came across a French novel entitled *Les dimanches de Mademoiselle Beaunon [The Sundays of Miss Beaunon]*.

As I told you, I was undecided and running away from my own memories. I clung to trivial things and was addicted to loafing about and getting lost in the streets of Paris, looking for a means to enable me to stay in the city and cut off my relations to my past and my country. As I was passing time walking on one of the sidewalks along the Seine River and thumbing used books for sale, I came across this novel. I knew nothing about Jacques Laurent, its author, but some chapter titles drew my attention: "Miss Beaunon and Spirituality," "Miss Beaunon and Drugs," "Miss Beaunon and Sex" . . . I read a few pages and liked the atmosphere of the story.

I returned early to my hotel to read the novel in solitude. Miss Beaunon works as a secretary at a certain establishment and she is in love with her boss, Paul Bache, but does not tell him anything, nor does she make him aware of her feelings toward him. Everyone at the establishment thinks she is a virgin and a recluse but, in fact, she has an abundant sex life of her own. Every Sunday she goes to the Rodin Museum or to the Louvre in order to capture a man to sleep with, then to withdraw from any continued relationship or further meeting with him. She washes her hands of the Sunday adventure and returns to her apartment and habits, and to receiving her granddaughter, Yolande, who works at an airline company. One Sunday, Miss Beaunon captures Olivier Gréard using her technique, which gradually moves from showing interest in details to uttering daring and sometimes insolent comments on the positions of the sculptured bodies exuding lust and eroticism. She finds pleasure in concealing her identity and withdrawing from her personality in order to surrender herself for a short time to an absolute sensuousness and to invent, while under its spell, other traits of her personality and life every time.

She enjoys the embarrassment she and her partner feel as they suddenly move from watching Rodin's bare statues to entering the state of nakedness of their own bodies that have been clothed a moment earlier. Gréard is about to divorce his wife when Miss Beaunon lures him to a small hotel where he usually reserves a room for his brother when visiting Paris. This experience for him, therefore, is not merely a transient one, especially as the beauty of Miss Beaunon's naked body and her brilliant performance in bed make him cling to her and express a desire to develop their relationship. But she knows how to get rid of him and she gives him information having nothing to do at all with her real life. A week after that meeting, she feels a desire to see him again, contrary to her custom, but she has torn up the note containing his address. Meanwhile, Gréard is in turn searching for her in vain in the telephone directory. Miss Beaunon realizes that she can no longer live a contented solitary life as she has done for twenty-five years, especially after the death of her boss whom she has loved silently. She tries to love two cats and tolerate their continuous quarrels. She moves to live outside Paris. But all that does not ward off the weight of boredom and the harshness of solitude. In turn, Gréard is searching for her all over Paris and writing his memoirs using the sweetest words to speak to her—until, one day, he sees her by accident in the street . . .

I will not tell you all the details of this novel, because what interests me in it is the personality of Miss Beaunon and the method she followed to attract men in order to ease her boredom and to satisfy her sexual curiosity with their nakedness.

I reread the novel again and again, and became attached to Miss Beaunon and her devilish idea. Before sleeping, I found I closed my eyes to recall her image in my mind using the author's description of her. But I did not succeed in putting an angelic face on an elegant body that could cause erotic excitement to those whom Miss Beaunon targeted. Her lips must have been full, her eyes must have penetrated men's clothing to set on their bodies underneath, despite her seemingly neutral look. I would continue to invent her image and give it various colors, then I would be driven to compare her image with myself: Don't I, too, have a streak of innocence wrapped in an ever-burning sensuousness like a fire under ashes?

At times, while deeply engrossed in identifying with Miss Beaunon's personality, I compared my room with the one at the hotel in which she slept with Gréard. I even almost determined it was the same room, for it was situated on the right side of the ground floor of the hotel, had a little dressing table, a washbowl, and a bidet behind a wooden partition covered with red fabric. From the window came the sound of women's heels knocking more sharply and more regularly than men's on the pavement— exactly as in the novel. I continued to fidget in bed until a late hour, when my hands would sneak into my pajamas to play with my clitoris and fondle my breasts and help my roused body join Miss Beaunon's heavy breathing and Gréard's raving words as they were about to have orgasm.

One day I got up ready to implement Miss Beaunon's plan. I felt I was impelled by a certain refreshing openness within me to move and abandon my escape from myself. I needed to ensure my stay in Paris by a method that depended on my youth and beauty, for all other doors seemed to be closed. I made my first visit to the Rodin Museum in order to get acquainted with the place and I bought a few books analyzing the art of sculpture and speaking about Rodin's life. At the same time, I wanted to be sure of what Miss Beaunon said about museums being the best places to meet and to organize adventures with peace of mind, for in them we are not in a hurry but rather move in parallel and continue to move and to switch neighbors, contrary to what happens in a theater as you watch a movie or a play. In a museum, we look together at the same statues and sculptures and we form impressions that can rise to our lips in words; we look at faces next to us and our eyes meet spontaneously, then move on, to meet again at another statue; and we begin to have the illusion that we know one another. Miss Beaunon could in this manner distinguish the kinds of men who visited museums alone and she could slowly select the one who would be the target of her attack.

Three days later I returned to the Rodin Museum, ready to embark on the new experience. I let my hair down on my shoulders, put on light makeup to suit the personality of the student I decided to be that day, and I wore a blue silk blouse and jeans, a plush violet coat, and a deep yellow woolen scarf that my mother Ghaylana had brought me as a present on her latest return from Spain. The visitors that morning were a few and among them there was only one man by himself. He was an elegantly dressed Japanese with a stern look whose age was difficult to guess. I thought to myself, "There is no way to withdraw now. It's only an experience and it does not need to be successful, for Miss Beaunon herself often returned empty-handed after her tour of the museum." I began to come closer to him until we came to watch the same statue. We exchanged looks as I turned and lingered, sometimes bending to look into the statue's crotch that was not visible at first sight. From time to time, I stopped and took out a small notebook and a pencil from my handbag, and began to write some notes (this was a procedure I had thought of earlier and it was an addition of mine to Miss Beaunon's plan). I began to follow my Japanese prey stealthily in preparation for my attack, and I noticed that he cast looks at me as though I had entered the area of his attention. Let me then attack before the opportunity is lost. We were near a statue whose title was *La Méditation*. I began turning around it, pretending I was surprised and purposely bumping into the Japanese man's back to mutter an apology and continue scrutinizing parts of the statue and writing notes about it.

After a short while, I stood next to him and muttered as though I were talking to myself, "This is strange. It seems to me that Rodin wants to deceive us by selecting such a title, isn't that so?"

He answered me in broken French, "What title do you mean, Miss?"

I smiled as I explained to him that Rodin gave that statue the title of *La Méditation* while it actually embodied an internal tension that the bronze could hardly contain, and that the deeper we examined it the more we felt the contagion of suppressed violence and explosion in ourselves.

He shook his head, saying, "Oh! That's right. I haven't paid attention to that."

Inspired by an idea that had occurred to Miss Beaunon, I added, "Perhaps this was intentional on the part of Rodin. He usually chose soothing titles in order not to expose himself to those who looked at his works."

Smiling with excessive politeness, he said, "Perhaps. Are you studying art, Miss?"

"More exactly, I am preparing a study on the works of Rodin."

He shook his head, showing greater interest. I seized the opportunity to move the dialogue to the artistic structure of another statue, pretending to write some notes, and I came closer to him again to whisper some other impression of mine. He walked by me as though baffled by my comments, most of which I had formerly memorized.

As we ended our tour and were near the museum's snack bar, I heard myself saying to him, "I'm thirsty. Would you allow me to offer you something to drink?"

He said, embarrassed, "On the contrary. I was thinking of inviting you."

I said, laughing, "You can invite me to something else. But it is my duty to be first to invite you as a guest in France."

At the café, I began to steer the conversation in order to explore his personality and know the extent of his readiness for adventure.

I said to him, pretending to be spontaneous, "After seeing Rodin's statue, I feel a burning electricity in my body and an irresistible desire to touch and feel things and bodies around me. Don't you?"

"Oh . . . What you say is true. As for me, the subject of touching depends on the body of a beautiful woman like you."

I burst out laughing, purposely prolonging my laughter, and I said as I pointed to him with my index finger, "I had not imagined you were a lover of women's beauty to this extent, for your manner rather suggests dignity."

"We, in Japan, are sensualists and spiritualists at the same time. We hardly differentiate between the two domains. Perhaps our excessive devotion to work is what sometimes conceals our sensualism and our lust."

"I find that your physiques excite the sensibility of the more rational women."

He bent his head down, joining his palms together, to thank me for my praise, meanwhile looking at my eyes and face and smiling.

We resumed our conversation and I learned that he was a businessman who had come to Paris on holiday and that he would not have had this holiday if the government had not lately decided that the Japanese, and especially businessmen, should go abroad during their vacations in order to spend some of their savings. As for me, I claimed that I was from Marseille, that my name was Yolande, that I had lost my husband in a car accident a year ago, and that I consequently preferred to occupy myself with studying art, in which I was interested before my marriage. Our conversation lasted until one o'clock, when Onto Hakara (that was his name) suggested that we have our lunch together. Naturally, I did not hesitate for a moment to accept his invitation, and I added that I hoped to receive him in my home in Marseille, if he had the time for that. During our lunch, I was thinking of an intelligent way, worthy of Miss Beaunon's inventive stratagems, to give me the opportunity to slip into Hakara's warm bed with him.

While we were preparing to leave the restaurant, I said to him in a calculated spontaneity, "I'll be deprived of my nap today because the friends hosting me live in the suburbs and I don't want to lose what remains of my day in the metro's underground tunnels." He said with extreme civility, "I'm staying at the Des Marronniers Hotel not far from here, and I'll be happy if you will share my nap with me, for I, too, can't dispense with it."

In his room he gave me a kimono made of fine cloth with plant designs. He excused himself because he wanted to take a shower. When he came out, he had a white bath towel wrapped around him and he started the ritual of bending his head and gesturing reverently that often appealed to me when watching Japanese movies. In turn I entered the bathroom to take a shower and when I came out, I began to imitate his bending laughingly. He corrected my movements and we soon resorted to touching and caressing each other. After saying a few words praising my harmonious body and my firm breasts, Onto Hakara hesitated a little, then said, "I'd like to show you a medical certificate saying I don't have any contagious diseases, especially AIDS, and I'd like if you . . ."

I interrupted, "Of course, but I don't have my medical documents with me, for I didn't have in mind an adventure of this kind, had it not been for your kindness and attractiveness. Can you therefore use a condom, if that doesn't bother you?"

Matters proceeded to their end, although my response was not at its climactic best after we took off our clothes. His smooth skin with its neutral yellow color and excessive clinging to his bones seemed to me devoid of any attractiveness. I passed my hand on it from top to bottom but did not feel any roughness to excite me. But the nudity of Rodin's statues and the specter of Miss Beaunon urged me to go ahead and achieve success in my new experience. Before we parted, I promised to contact him before his departure, and I gave him a phony address in Marseille. Of course, I never thought of contacting him again, in respect for Miss Beaunon's tradition and also because I was searching for men of another kind.

I returned happily to my hotel and gave myself up to fanciful dreams and possibilities. I thought to myself, "This path can take me to a safe haven. Why not? I have to determine what I want, I mean, I have to acquaint myself with what will save me from this temporary situation."

Images and suppositions were mixed in my mind and I decided to go back to reading *Les dimanches de Mademoiselle Beaunon* and the books on Rodin's life and art, for from them salvation would come as my intuition whispered.

I will spare you, dear al-'Ayshuni, the details of other uncommon and exciting meetings at the Rodin Museum. But I will tell you about the day I met Matthias Pedal, whose wife I became three months ago. Yes, my name has become Fatima Pedal instead of Fatima Quraytis. Some time had to pass before I became accustomed to this new name.

On that day—it was a Sunday—I went to the Rodin Museum having adopted the personality of a postgraduate student, after having tried several other personalities such as a feudal lord's daughter, the delegate of the Moroccan Museum of Plastic Arts (I know that it does not exist and you often complained of that, so I wanted to remove this injustice), the owner of an art gallery in Casablanca . . . The ecstasy of Miss Beaunon's game had begun to lose its attraction, because the meetings did not offer me any straw to cling to. On the contrary, I sometimes had difficult moments during my private meetings with some of the men I lured. I met with sadistic situations that frightened me and with masochistic ones that baffled me, and I found myself immersed in experiences that had harsh surprises and in sexual relations that exiled my body from me more and more.

On that Sunday, I moved without enthusiasm, having decided to be cautious in making a choice among the solitary men.

I looked around with slow deliberation, examining their features, and I followed their movements and tried to read their faces. Not far from Rodin's statue *The Kiss,* I saw him, with his white round face, his ruddy cheeks, and his blond hair combed frontward. He was leaning on a wall and moving his look among the statues in the hall with a happy smile on his lips. I did not hesitate to come close to him as though a hidden hand were pushing me toward him from behind. I took out my notebook to pretend I was recording some notes; then I looked in his direction, muttering:

"This representation of the kiss surpassed both reality and imagination . . . Each time I see *The Kiss* it suggests new feelings to me."

"Isn't that so, Miss?" he answered with exuberance and joy. "I have a similar feeling, too, although I haven't visited the museum for almost a year."

I was overwhelmed with satisfaction, for he appeared to be a Frenchman, to judge by his manner of speaking and his way of expressing himself, which was sincere and spontaneous. In order not to appear as a mere ordinary visitor, I added after an interval:

"I find, though, that the statue does not represent the invisible dimension which the kiss incites in the embracing bodies . . ."

It was as if he were surprised by my observation. So he gave the statue another look; then he said:

"Perhaps . . . But I think that what you are talking about is created in different ways in the souls of the onlookers."

I added, in order to prolong the conversation and keep him at my side:

"What interests me is that the statue should, in its structure and material, contain what represents the dynamic quality of an experience, especially when the matter is related to a kiss, which is, before anything else, a declaration about a transformation in the chemistry of two bodies and an inauguration of a movement that does not cease . . ."

He said, hesitantly, "In this case, we should perhaps demand that the sculptor get out of the limits of sculpture and use other elements that represent this dynamism."

"Why not? There are attempts, perhaps you have heard of, by painters and sculptors who use motors and metal leaves and twigs to represent the dynamism of statues or paintings."

"Oh! I've seen examples of them but I did not feel any response to them within me, for they don't leave the imagination free to move."

I had to withdraw from my position so that he would not feel I contradicted his taste, so I said:

"I agree with you in this respect . . . Rodin's power is amazing, although it may appear to suppress its own dynamism."

I quickly moved the conversation to Rodin's love life and his story with Camille Claudel: "I don't think you're going to defend his harsh treatment of Camille?"

"I don't know the details of this relationship but I've read a positive review of a movie about their love and it is currently showing in movie theaters. I intend to see it tonight."

"What a strange coincidence! This movie is also on my program for today!"

He said, smiling, "Then we can go together to see it, if there is no objection on your part?"

I pretended to hesitate for a moment, then I said, "It will be my pleasure. Let me invite you to a cup of tea at the museum's snack bar."

I was overwhelmed by an inner joy because an intuitive feeling told me my relationship with Matthias would be different. I decided not to hurry in executing my familiar plan and to behave this time as if I lived an experience open to all possibilities and it was in my interest to let the element of confusion work. Our conversation touched on our private lives, so I began the questions. He answered, saying that his name was Matthias Pedal, that he ran a company in Paris to produce leather clothes, and that he did that to please his mother, who had asked him to take over the job from his father, who died two years ago. He said that his mother lived in Menton and came to visit him from time to time, and that he visited her now and then, for he could not live far away from her, especially after he had spent ten years with her without interruption during his father's residence in Guadeloupe after their return from Morocco . . ."

"Morocco?" I interrupted.

"Yes. I was born there, because my father worked in the French administration during the Protectorate period. We lived in a little town called Petitjean, which is now called Sidi Qasem."

"I know that well, for I am from Morocco."

"What a happy surprise! Is what you tell me true?"

"Absolutely. And my name is Fatima Quraytis and I was born in Fez."

As he was telling about his childhood in Sidi Qasem and his visits to Meknas, Fez, and Casablanca, I was arranging in my mind what I would tell him about my life, amended so that he would not escape from my net, especially because he was pleased that I was from Morocco. I thought, "Praise be to Him Who makes hearts tender! The homeland that I've done my best to shirk and erase from my memory with all those in it has come to my aid!"

"My childhood in Morocco was wonderful and it is impossible for me to forget it," Matthias repeated, his eyes wandering as though he was recalling the green pastures and fields, the sturdy olive trees and tall willows, and the minarets thrusting their heads toward heaven.

He spoke and I examined his round face and his permanently ruddy cheeks, and I was happy with Matthias's sincere tone bordering sometimes on naïvety. He repeated his mother's name and iterated his constant yearning for Morocco. Despite the success of his company and the luxury of his life, he did not feel happy in Paris. His mother feared that he might fall prey to bad relationships and so she kept an eye on his private life, but he was looking for another life that would give him equilibrium and please his mother at the same time. Oh, how complicated life was, he said.

"Indeed, my golden goose," I thought to myself. "Life is very complicated and you are a rare kind of being as it seems, the kind I was looking for until I've almost given up in despair . . . I am ready to serve you and devote myself to obeying you and spoiling you and representing the image of the tawny, ardent woman exclusively occupied with giving pleasure to her man . . . I can even play to your mother the role of the submissive person obeying her orders and tolerating her imbecility . . ."

Then I would restrain myself and whisper, "Haste is waste. We rather have to let the goose become well done on a light fire so that its taste may be delightful, 'finger-licking delicious' as people say in our country."

When my turn came to tell my life story, I did not hesitate to put my father and mother to death. I claimed I had been an orphan for more than ten years and that my uncle had sponsored me, so I completed my university education but jobs were not available. My uncle thought of marrying me off to a married merchant who wanted to enliven his middle age. I refused and felt I was suffocating. Only the image of Paris figured in my mind as a savior from the vulgar destiny about to be foisted on me . . . So I embarked on the adventure of coming to Paris but discovered difficulties that had not occurred to me. Yet I was determined to stay and create a life for myself that would spare me oppression and reification . . . Then I asked, "Can you give me a job at your company?"

I laughed after my last sentence and he laughed too.

He said, "You rather deserve much better work than that, work that is commensurate with your education . . ."

He hesitated a little, then added, ". . . and your beauty."

"Thanks," I said, having called upon all my inner forces to make my cheeks blush in embarrassment. I lowered my eyelids and looked shyly at the table for a few moments that I prolonged as much as I could.

(As I am now writing about those moments, the possibility that I was implementing an idea expressed by Miss Beaunon jumps to my mind. I stopped writing and referred to the novel but did not find anything confirming my behavior. Perhaps I read that idea in another novel; or else calling upon my cheeks to blush and prolonging my look at the table with lowered eyelids are additions I made to the personality of Miss Beaunon, then I borrowed them from her after I had added them to her!)

In the theater, as we watched Camille Claudel in the movie, I was careful to choose the scene that would justify my touching him. The opportunity came when scenes began to show Camille secluded in her studio, having declared war on Rodin. Her defiance was wonderful and frightening. Rodin had chosen his own established life and reputation and had turned away from Camille's love and infatuation with sculpture; so she felt that he was using her and stealing her work and that her infinite love for him clashed with his strong desire for general success and the recognition of his genius by official circles. She found herself alone, undecided, unable to reach the heavens of love and creativity, and incapable of withdrawing. It was impossible for her to back off. But the pain of being jilted and the disappointment with the lover and master would make her fall into the abyss of despair and madness. She was in her ground-floor room, where she created statues that had her features and airs. The press began to speak about her but she felt she was besieged and that an essential thing had broken within her. She became addicted to drinking and went deep into a labyrinth of hallucination she could not bear. Like an unruly pony, she began to smash her statues. Her nerves out of control, she smashed everything in sight around her. She screamed, having lost her human features despite her exceeding beauty. She smashed and screamed.

I seized this dramatic moment to touch Matthias's elbow, muttering, "Poor woman!"

His hand quickly moved to hold mine, his fingers conveying to me reassuring and loving touches. And I did not let go of his hand until the end of the movie.

Meetings between Matthias and me became regular. He started inviting me to his apartment in the Fifteenth Arrondissement and I found myself fully adopting the role of lady of the house. I would cook Moroccan dishes as though to recall a memory common to Matthias and myself. He liked what I cooked and was pleased to see me with two braids and wearing a *mansuriyya* tunic as I received him in the evening on his return from work. I made a point of postponing sexual relations between us; and he, too, was not in a hurry. I was looking for another rhythm of life after my feverish escapades of chasing men at the Rodin Museum and my being driven by hallucinations that made me live inhuman situations qualified by the frenzy of successfully obtaining a worthy catch. It was difficult for me to regain the natural behavior I had before frequenting the Rodin Museum. It is as though the temporary role I played erased my first personality and abolished my stored-up memories to make of me a woman fixated on one idea and one aim that consumed all my attention. When our relations became regularized, I made a big effort to get rid of my crazy attempts to look for a man to save me from my predicament. I had never thought that the procedure prescribed by Miss Beaunon would take hold of me to that extent. So I gave myself up to cooking enthusiastically in order to revive my memory and gradually regain ordinary relationships with people and things. Matthias's behavior was helpful, for he prolonged the period of ambiguous allusions and shy flirtations. And when we began having sex, a certain closeness had been woven between us, and his warm emotions toward me made me adopt modesty and limit the freedom of my body during sex.

I began to make myself accustomed to discovering the qualities of his white body and hairless chest and to imagine unfamiliar worlds in his blue eyes. I did my best to make him happy and attach him to my effervescent body holding a variety of experiences. I gradually began to relinquish my modesty and let my tongue, from time to time, daringly flicker over sensitive points of Matthias's body. His sighs called for more of the same in appreciation and my body in turn gave up its false modesty, and its pores opened to absorb Matthias's kisses and his nectar. Yet despite the regularity of our bodies' rhythm and Matthias's attachment to me and to the lover's role I wholly took, I continued to be filled with anxiety so long as his mother, Madame Chantal, had not yet approved her son's choice of me.

Finally the day of my meeting with Madame Chantal arrived. I had waited impatiently for it and I feared it. I observed Matthias as he prepared for it, taking into consideration his mother's mentality and her temperament, until I agreed to go with him to visit her in Menton. Her long, stern face with its wrinkles covered with layers of creams and powders, her invasive look, her silver bracelets and anklets, the bright colors of her clothes . . . all that was fully integrated within the ambiance of the house and its furniture. It was an old stone house, perched on a hill, surrounded by willows, rubber trees, linden trees, and creeping plants of all colors clinging to the house's surface and pillars. The large drawing room in which she received us was cluttered with old armchairs and tables, statuettes and copper objects, wooden armoires, ancient pots hanging on the walls, and three wall clocks that reminded me of the clock at our home in Fez . . . and then there were the cats and dogs. In the midst of all that, Madame Chantal appeared to be the hub around which everything turned. She hardly stopped talking. Her sentences were decisive and exuded derision and sarcasm. Her conversation was peppered with allusions to the good old days in Guadeloupe and Morocco. I was at a loss and did not know how to greet her and felt I was shaking as I stretched my hand toward her, but she pulled me to her to kiss me on my cheek. I blushed, my eyelids fluttered, and I was terribly embarrassed. That, after a while, made her say in French, "Elle est mignonne, ta marocaine" (She's cute, your Moroccan girl).

I muttered in an agitated voice, "Thank you, Madam."

In the afternoon, Madame Chantal's friends began to arrive in her drawing room; they were old and yet pretended they were still young. Creams concealed the wrinkles of their faces, their lipstick shone brightly, their jewelry glittered, and their fashionable clothes corrected their figures wrecked by time.

At first, I was naturally the center of their attention and the object of their comments but they later moved to their favorite gossip and reviewed the news of the town and the world. A considerable part of their conversation was about a new cream to remove wrinkles.

Madame Chantal said, "Did you know of the antiwrinkle cream invented by the American dermatologist Gormby?" She then embarked on enumerating its many benefits.

"Has it arrived at our drugstores?" asked one of the ladies.

"I was told it will arrive some time next week. Its effect is guaranteed, it seems, for Professor Gormby spent many years doing research to make it and he affirmed to the press conference held to present the cream that it will give any woman using it twenty years of additional youth."

"Oh! What a happy piece of news!"

When Madame Chantal felt that the subject was exhausted, she jumped to another, always in a confident tone and a language accompanied by nudges and prickly remarks. And so, she moved from the youth-granting cream to the qualities of Madonna, the singer.

"I saw a wonderful movie yesterday about the life of the ravishing Madonna . . . She is really strange and exciting. Imagine, in one scene at the Olympia theater, she uncovered her breasts and threw her slip to the audience!"

One of the ladies present interrupted, "True, she's ravishing but without any decency."

Madame Chantal retorted, "Look who's talking of decency!"

Bursts of laughter ensued; then black tea and delicious pastries were served, followed by alcoholic drinks to whet the appetite before Madame Chantal's coterie dispersed.

I was there, with them, participating in their laughter and listening intently to what was being said; but my imagination carried me afield from time to time and I pictured myself as a future part of this assembly, keeping company with Matthias and his mother and getting accustomed to the social ways of the old ladies attempting to look youthful and to their conversations and acting. I imagined myself serving Madame Chantal devotedly in order to win her trust and waiting for the day when the house would be turned to Matthias and me, and hoping the dream I had had since my days in the halls of the Rodin Museum would come true.

That first night spent at Madame Chantal's house, I could not sleep until the early hours of the morning. The strokes of the wall clocks with their long-echoing, sonorous sound in the silence of the large house reminded me of my childhood home in Fez, regularly filled with the sound of the brown, rectangular wall clock dominating the large room. How did I forget that rhythm? Did I really forget it? It was as though time had not changed, yet I felt I was at a crucial threshold that I looked forward to crossing in order to end my relation to that past, which I was determined to forget.

As my letter approaches its end, perhaps you grin to express your disappointment with the former Fatima Quraytis, currently Fatima Pedal, who lived with you several wingèd nights and morns, and who saw in your words and lines invisible worlds that you ran after, panting, before returning to your meditations and dreams. I was happy near you, although I knew I was about to discover another reality, one I am now engaged in with fear and apprehension. Where did all those feelings, impulses, and whims go that were my life? The whole world to me is now summarized in this project that I am trying to artfully swindle out of Matthias and his mother. We got married, but I live a life of constant alert.

One month after our marriage, I remember I woke up late. It was Sunday and Matthias had gone to visit his mother in the south. The clear, sunny weather tempted me to go out: I love the streets of Paris when they are almost empty and have regained their complex, architectural features through the play of light and long shadows. I wandered aimlessly and suddenly I felt I was completely empty of all vitality. I was besieged by that state of mind which I experienced after I returned from the Riviera and during my regular visits to the Rodin Museum. I became dizzy, so I sat down on a public bench on the sidewalk. I remained seated for a long while, then I heard the bells of a church and I thought of trying to confess to a priest all that I had done in the recent months.

I returned to my apartment to rest and wait for the evening. But the idea of confession continued to buzz in my head. So I put a scarf on my head and went to the nearest church. There were two women waiting at the confessional in which the priest sat. When my turn came, I found that I was in the state of loss I had experienced during the past months. A feverish hallucination took hold of me and I spoke about closed horizons, meaningless

life, sexual sins and adventures that often lured me with the illusion of renewal through pleasure . . . I ended my confession saying, "Father, I feel suffocated, I feel that I am besieged and that
nothing lives within me or around me."

After a short silence, I heard the priest's voice saying, "My
daughter, let me remind you of what St. Paul said: 'Who thought
that life would begin from the top of a forgotten rock in the middle of the sea?' "

I stretched out my hand to him through the window and
touched his warm hand, which made me tremble from the bottom of my feet to my navel. I almost felt impelled to open the
curtain and say to him, "Take me now into your lap, in this holy
confessional that I want to consider as the rock on which I will
be born again." But I thought of the scandal and of Matthias and
his fortune, part of which will become mine; so I felt I was far
from the spirit of adventure that had fired my whims formerly.

As I told you at the beginning of this letter, I am writing to
you from Menton, where we will spend the summer with my
mother-in-law (May you be as fortunate), Madame Chantal,
who takes pleasure in talking for hours on end while I listen to
her attentively . . . I am writing to you as the news of the
hostages released in Baghdad fills the emptiness of this summer in
the media; as Pérez de Cuellar, with his miserable-looking face
always suggesting he is about to cry, announces he is increasingly
optimistic; as hundreds of Albanians are besieged by the Italian
police lest they should infiltrate into the country as if they were
an epidemic; as the security forces in Madagascar fire at thou-
sands of demonstrators . . . Yet, talk about a new world order
continues, an order that will be applied and realized by the
United States of America . . .

Where am I in relation to all this? Nothing moves me, for I am like an oyster shell closed shut on one hope: Madame Chantal's death so that Matthias may inherit her fortune and the formation of a fetus in my womb guaranteeing my share of this fortune. And who knows? Something may happen and take away Matthias, and I will then enjoy what remains of my life comfortably, without material worries, as one person among innumerable women and men living on the crumbs of certain rich folks in exchange for services they do or roles they play unwillingly.

Is my fate different from my mother's? Perhaps, especially if my illusions come true. Then you will not be able to deny that I knew how to use stratagems intelligently in order to insure my future, how to depend on courses in "planning" and administration that I took at the university and on ways I learned from my readings . . . Yes, O artist, knowledge is light, and what a light!

If my plans and illusions come true, I will think of visiting you if your life journey on earth still continues. I will then see what time has made of you. Before that, I don't think I will write to you again or think of visiting you or mother Ghaylana. I don't even want you to tell her about this letter, for there is no longer anything that ties me to her and I don't want to cause her further pain. That's what I am now—without illusions, without emotions—a robot moving by an internal mechanism.

I wait for the realization of my illusions because I am unable to commit suicide. Of the others, all the others, even of you who inflamed my body and soul for some time, my memory has kept nothing—no features, no words, nothing. I feel my memory is empty, smooth.

I wanted to end this letter by telling you about a strange scene I saw on television, but it slips my mind amid hundreds of other scenes shown on the small screen, to which I have become addicted. This scene attracted my attention because it represented my state . . . What state? I must remember, I must lure it back, perhaps it will come . . . Aha! The scene has come back. It was in a program showing the progress achieved by artificial intelligence. This intelligence is no longer limited to computer programming and offering answers to possible questions but, as I saw on television, it can even expect and imagine dialogue between a man and a woman meeting at an evening party: a female mannequin wearing an evening gown with a low-cut neckline showing the upper part of her body and a male mannequin wearing a dark blue suit with a red necktie. He bows to her as he greets her and she responds in a gentle voice coming from within her body as her facial features move to form a sweet smile . . . They both raise their glasses to drink a toast and the dialogue continues in a "rational," "very rational" language, as the anchorman assures us from behind the small screen and invites us to listen to a sample of that dialogue . . .

This is how I see myself now: a body within a mannequin, run from behind a curtain by an artificial intelligence that makes me move by certain calculations and controls. Meanwhile, I can hardly believe what I see: all the brilliant memories lose their light and seem pale like the echo of mirrors, their glow fades and dies. Who said that heroism dies after it runs its course and time extinguishes its luster? It does not matter who said that, because it applies to all that moves illusions within us . . . Can you create a new heroism for us, other illusions, other dreams, O artist?

Excerpts from Al-ʿAyshuni's Notebooks

In the Morning

Some cities knew no more than one owner, one lover, one history . . . But Tangier was familiar with numerous lovers and with great men of history. The city is not real except to the extent that we envelop its myth with consistency and continuity. Sired by the imagination of the Greek giant Anteus, son of Neptune, and bearing its first name Tingis, it received the Phoenicians, the Carthaginians, and the Romans before it hosted those coming from the Arab East: ʿUqba ibn Nafiʿ, then Musa ibn Nusayr. It wore the apparel of the Moravids, the Almohads, and the Merinids before being mortgaged to the Portuguese and the Spaniards. In the seventeenth century, it was presented on a plate of gold as a dowry of a Portuguese princess who married King Charles II of England in 1661. Mulay Ismaʿil regained the city-gift but, starting from this century, it has been a gift to all races and peoples: A city in common? A woman gone to perdition? Space that can't bear constraints and boundaries?

Isn't all this plurality of fashions, histories, and languages of its residents what brings it close to the soul that always yearns for more than one costume and one mask, for more than one love and one body, for more than one language and one space?

Just before Evening

Tangier to me is almost always associated with light, with sunshine, with clarity emanating from the Mediterranean . . . even if I have, for long, loved its winter nights rooted firmly in my mind, when I was fond of making the rounds of bars and walking in the pouring rain.

After all this long time spent in it, I don't think I have absorbed all its vibrations and radiance.

I always find myself at the beginning of discovering it, for it is like a beautiful woman who yields her hidden treasures with calculation. Its ascending and descending alleys, its buildings with neoclassical architecture, its hills distributed in a vast expanse in which the shapes of its homes jostle one another in mosaic patterns with chaos and intertwining disposition . . . all this overcrowded appearance is new to Tangier, yet it creates its own urban din. And despite everything, Tangier to me remains associated in my childhood memory with semi-empty streets and with bright light flooding the scene with warm rhythm and inaugural song . . . Each time I say that I am almost blended with it and have captured it in my paintings, some invisible blindfold conceals it from me.

At Night

Luxury hotels have become many in the era of Moroccan tourism but the Minzah Hotel remains the meeting-place of Tangier's elite and its wealthy visitors. Faces have changed in it but the function of the Minzah has hardly changed. Ever since it was built by the Scottish Lord Bute in 1930 with its Andalusian style and its garden full of the most beautiful trees and flowers, it has been attracting representatives of high society . . . Within its walls, deals have been made, friendships formed, adventures undertaken, and spy reports written. It is an indispensable mirror for those on top who try to feel the pulse of politics and economics, and who want to gather family secrets and information coming from overseas.

And ever since Moroccans have become proprietors of the hotel, including a minister-for-life, the Minzah has regained its ascendancy and its lure for those looking for state secrets. Everyone goes to it to satisfy a certain desire, but those who know the history of this hotel well say that what will always be remembered about it are its parties of revelry, shameless pleasure, and frenzied dancing.

As for me, I remain attached to scenes at the Minzah just before sunset in the summer, when the garden and the swimming pool become a basin full of light diffused by the warm sun . . . light overflowing with charm, tenderness, transparency and inundating things and souls with calm and incandescence.

Before Dawn

A whole week passed without seeing Ghaylana, who, suddenly, stopped visiting me. When I had a feeling that I might lose her, I was overtaken by a state of constant grief and unimaginable suffering: grief would choke me at the throat, in the back of my nose, in my eye sockets, and it would make crying impossible to the extent of suffocating me and taking my breath away. It was a state comparable to the expectation of my own foretold death. To lose her, to lose all my beautiful moments and illusions, means that I will return to being an ordinary person like everyone else. I am unable to analyze the situation but I fear this permanent grief.

At Night

After Ghaylana's disappearance, my world has become cold. I have become suddenly unable to receive any message. It is as if I had undergone a lobotomy operation, very much like a frog whose brain has been removed, so it continues to hop for a short while on the marble slab of the dissection table, while its head is empty of the world and of things—it moves but it is empty.

How can I regain the world?

I should make myself believe that I can control reality again by firmly reestablishing relationships with my surroundings. Everything around me seems vast and distant, utterly changed despite its same external appearance. Will it be sufficient for me to broaden my interest in people and their problems, in history and its checkered snares, in politics and their surprises? Will that restore the motivation I have lost?

I have no desire to abandon the life with which I am familiar but I feel that, within this familiar cocoon, I am indolent, viscous, afraid of a grief that tears my innards apart.

In the Afternoon

My mother talks to me in her biologically inherited language and she makes me tremble with emotion. She tells me about her daily battles in Suq Barra [the Outer Market], about rising prices, about people who have no more patience and can endure no longer . . . I absorb her words, dumbfounded and ecstatic. "What's the matter, boy?" she asks. I become aware that I have been distracted. I mutter that everything is fine. She smiles and adds, "That girl, Ghaylana, has made you lose your head. Why don't you marry her? It's true, her beauty makes one fall madly in love with her."

Ghaylana asked me more than once to take her to our village to visit my relatives, but I declined without knowing the reason. I lately thought that I might find there what I imagined to be the lost roots. But no, for the worms are here, eating away at my head, gnawing on my innards, and I can't find rest at a point of departure until I dissipate these doubts, until I find answers, even provisional ones.

I feel I am distributed between a foggy imagined world difficult to reach and another that is a mixture of gametes and spindrift blown to the four winds.

In the Evening

I remember the night Joséo died: one would think he was preparing to go on a short trip, as he did from time to time. He was lying in bed, struggling to keep smiling despite the pain that squeezed his whole body. He gave me an envelope containing his will and checks in my name. He had thought of everything to insure my material future. He wished me good luck, then stopped talking. Moments later, he was extinguished, still retaining a certain smile. Tears welled up in my eyes and I continued to cry for a long time before I thought of executing his wish to be buried in Tangier.

With Joséo's death, my alienation increased. How will I face the world through my paintings? This beautiful house has become mine and my balance at the bank insures sufficient income for my monthly expenses. With painting as my horizon and my destiny, I have nothing but my brush and colors, and my many intertwining ideas and dreams that can hardly stand still.

In the Morning

A friendly relationship ties me to Muhammad Hadidesh, who is a guard at the Minzah Hotel. He excels in the art of effective speaking and is acquainted with famous foreign personalities frequenting the hotel. He told me that he had an affectionate relationship with Barbara Hutton, the wealthy woman who preferred to live in Tangier, "her paradise on earth." Beautiful and rich, she was enamored of the dolce vita, parties, and the company of famous men . . . And yet, as Hadidesh told me, she complained to him of loneliness and kept saying, "No one will know how miserable I've been." Hadidesh commented, "What do you want, brother? Neither money nor prestige will make you happy. Peace of mind is worth millions."

In the Afternoon

I became acquainted yesterday with a girl from Tangier who is a student at the University of Rabat. Exciting and impudent, her experience appears to be too big for her age. In the conversation, after a few drinks that made us congenial, she told me about an adventure she had five years ago when she was a student at the Spanish high school here in Tangier. A male friend of hers suggested to her that she invite some of her female friends so that a foreign photographer, paying a temptingly large sum of money, would be permitted to take a collective picture of them naked. The picture would be published abroad and no one here would know, but the budget for evening parties and going to dancing clubs would be abundantly insured for the girl and her friends. The meeting took place at the Cinco Minutos Bar and the photo-taking appointments became lucrative until the police got wind of the scandal. The girls did not spend much time in prison because they were said to be "deceived" minors, but the club owner was imprisoned for five years, then exiled from Tangier . . .

She spoke as if what she narrated had happened to somebody else. At the university, she does not believe in what she studies and that's why she searches continually for something else that suits her temperament. She wants to enjoy life, to be in evening parties, to respond to her own desires . . . Anything else is mere words blown by the wind.

I had read about this scandal and had heard about it when it took place in the 1970s. Everybody deplored these bad manners and condemned foreigners because they brought the seeds of depravity to our country. But my meeting with one of the "victims" left another impression on me: her audacity in selling her body was a means to express herself, for she was searching for something she did not find in what she heard, and yet it was taught day and night. Hence, it appears that what she did agreed with her own understanding of things.

In the Evening

I rarely enter a discussion about a big subject, especially with people I don't know well. At one of the cafés today, and in the

presence of painters, writers, and journalists, the future was dis-
cussed as well as current social change. The conversation flowed
with vehemence, diversity, and noise as though in a "general
forum." I was satisfied to be a listener. One young writer asked
for my opinion and I only gestured and smiled, indicating I did
not have an opinion on the subject. A short while later I felt a
sudden desire to say something, and I said to him, "The image of
change is not clear, for everyone imagines it to be achieved in his
way. I'm thinking of Tangier under the international regime. It
seems to me that it was more prosperous, although it depended
on foreign models at the time. Perhaps I'm saying this because I
benefitted from that situation by chance. I now miss that vitality
and that prosperity. Other than internal tourism in the summer,
stagnation is the rule now. In spite of many changes, interminable
celebrations, and announcements about future projects . . . the
image remains foggy, and what actually happens is far from the
declared intentions. Everyone now admits that we are in a bind,
even those who participated in bringing it about. At any rate, I'm
not one of those who make history and perhaps I'm one of those
who bear its consequences, but my material situation puts me in
a special situation. You may find me less optimistic than you because I have lived a longer time than you and learned by experience to distinguish between hope and illusion."

Early in the Morning

When I opened my eyes this morning, the remains of a strange
dream lingered in my memory. In a large garden, there were men
and women in evening dress standing in a long line, at the end of
which stood servants who offered them empty plates and mo-

tioned them to break them on iron blocks in front of them. I look at my dark blue suit that I am wearing and don't remember that I have one like it. I hesitate to break the plate, so the servant holds my hand to help me, always smiling, and offers me another plate and invites me to repeat the operation . . .

I don't remember that I ever attended such a ceremony but I recall an evening party in Madrid at the residence of a group of artists who drank red wine then threw the glasses against the wall to fly off in smitherines according to the old Russian tradition . . . Plates are akin to glasses and breaking them symbolizes gain and long life!

In the Evening

When I lived in Marrakesh, during my relationship with Kanza, I befriended a traditional barber in the old city. I went to him the first time to have him shave my beard, and during the conversation he asked me about my job. I said, "I'm a painter." He stopped shaving me, eyed me with a smile on his face, and said in a pleasant tone, "You're then an artist, sir? God bless you. Popular or modern art?"

From that day on, I went to the barber's from time to time, and I met there some of his friends who smoked pot and talked freely and used sharp sarcasm.

At Night

I have not painted for a whole week. I was beset by a sudden anxiety. In such situations, sex emerges to assault me with its dark shades and masks, and takes me to labyrinths to be lost in illusions. Women and sex take hold of all my senses. I can think of nothing but that. Everything is swallowed by this vehement sensation, and intercourse does not extinguish it because my desire is linked to my thinking of the ritual accompanying it, and of the relation of sex to life, death, loneliness, and communication . . .

Since my experience with Ghaylana, then with Kanza, sex has become for me a necessary ritual to achieve equilibrium and continuity, or rather to obtain a certainty completely different from the one inherited, a certainty that strengthens the illusion of freedom and of possessing the moment here and now.

But sometimes I feel as if I am emptied, so I no longer have that which ties me to what surrounds me. It is a fierce, animal feeling. Permanent erection, abolition of the other, and embodiment of pure sex. There is agonizing torment before the specter of a woman clad in silk appears and humanizes my looks and the impulses of my body. A woman enveloped in silk fascinates my sight and transforms my universe into a focal point condensing the others, women and men . . . A tender touch by her affects my whole body and my life is gradually resumed.

In the Afternoon

I wonder whether I am living a deep phase of my life, characterized by permanent tensions between being inclined to order and being attracted by chaos, between being fascinated and being anxious, between being uncertain and being submissive to tradition . . . Nothing I hear or read illumines for me this nebulous quality that enfolds everything. Perhaps we should learn how to interpret what happens in the vast tunnels of the unconscious, where bubbles appear that we find surprising.

Does it suffice that I find shelter in rejection, that I experience ecstasy in solitude: will it be enough, so that I may continue this voyage whose ship knows no haven to go to?

I have no answer to my question except what Rainer Maria Rilke said, "Asceticism is no solution, for it is a negative indication of desire."

In the Afternoon

In a conversation with a writer friend, he said to me, "We should search for another way to write, for we may free ourselves from one kind of rhetoric to imprison ourselves in another. The result is our inability to move the heart and mind of the reader. Changing our style and language is not sufficient. I, for one, stand perplexed before the question of sex. All that I think and build my conceptions on, as I observe people, reveals nothing but mirage.

"There is something in our sex life that crystallizes specific ways of behavior, mostly not understood. A man's relation with a woman puts me in an impasse when I write. What makes 'our' man reify the woman and practice sex with himself through her as though she were not a human being who has desires, who is independent, and who searches for shared pleasure? Does the cause of that go back to childhood and early upbringing? Or is it an expression of violence thrown off course?"

Then he added, "I have an impression that we are sexually starved, no matter how often we have sex. I know a married man who, to insure daily ejaculation [qadhf], had affairs with many other women; and yet his eyes continued to follow every female apparition and reveal his 'historic' starvation . . . We called him

Ejaculator [*Qadhafi*] and he was pleased with the 'revolutionary' connotation of this name!"

At Night

For a long time now, I have not been to the Minzah Hotel to have a drink, although Joséo often took me with him to its bar and garden, where he met with Tangier's international lovers and where languages and dialects mixed and men and women competed in elegance . . . The habitual visitors of the Minzah used to ignore everyone else; you would feel they alone lived in luxurious Tangier and they alone were the ones representing this wingèd city.

When I entered the Minzah this evening, at the end of a clear sunny day, I saw faces most of which I had not seen there before but they took me back forty years in time: American women of loud merriment, Spanish women of delicate features, French women of enigmatic appearance, men of all ages, Moroccans coming from the capital and from Casablanca putting on artificial airs of seriousness and vulgar elegance . . . The tunes of the piano coming from the bar were hardly heard in the garden, where all the people talked as though they were invited guests at a regular party. I saw Madame Rachelle, the owner of Les Colonnes bookstore, and she greeted me, saying aloud, "The famous French writer M—— is in town today and I want to introduce you to him. Don't disappear from my sight."

Laughter did not cease. I think that it is what creates the atmosphere of vitality and enjoyment and it is what reminds me of Tangier of the olden days. The difference may be that it was earlier the laughter of people who lived in Tangier, summer and winter, and who endowed the city with the glitter of "permanent" bliss. These people here come today in the summer for rest or in search of an image of the city recorded in books or to buy smuggled goods . . . But can a city live, love itself, without such laughter?

In the Afternoon

My relation to Kanza was cut off and I no longer visit Marrakesh but I think about her now and then. I think of her loneliness, her difficult conditions despite her immersion in political activities and women's meetings. It is not easy for a divorced woman to lead the life she wants, especially if she is like Kanza who rejects social conventions. Her voice comes to me from time to time on the telephone and our conversation appears extremely pleasant and cordial. For although we both know that our love relationship has come to an end, there continues to be some clinging to something beautiful, to a refreshing memory we don't want to lose . . . We cling to it despite our awareness that we belong to it no more.

At Night

Cling to your chaos, my heart, for order—any order—will grant you nothing but monotony and surrender and cocoon rottenness; it will deprive you of being fascinated by the brightness of morning, by the golden light of late afternoon, by the soft caress of the breeze; it will stand between you and the pleasure of walking on a narrow isthmus in response to a call from a bottomless abyss.

Chaos? Order?

At least, when you utter the word "chaos," that suggests jungles of meaning. As for order, how ugly is the austerity of its wrinkles!

To exclaim, "I'm happy," as I look at Tangier's azure sky while my heart overflows with beautiful despair—isn't this the climax of chaos?

In the Evening

When Fatima, Ghaylana's daughter, lived with me, I was bewildered by her: she intruded into my life in her capacity as the daughter of my sweetheart Ghaylana, she acted with charming maturity and sensitivity, she gave me to taste diverse kinds of pleasures of the flesh . . . then she refused to tell me anything about her life.

Her letter to me, a year and a half after she left (I received it yesterday), is what illuminates certain features of that fugitive face. I read and hardly believe: all that sensitivity, all that tornness, all that ability for devilish behavior! I am terrified at the numerous forms of violence that Fatima faces in France, using trickery and running after what I consider to be illusions, perhaps because I am one of those fortunate to have the bliss of being "established."

In the Afternoon

With Ghaylana at al-Ghanduri's Restaurant, I felt at first as though we were resuming our interrupted relationship. But her lost innocence and her new personality drew my attention to the numerous possibilities still existing in reality. Matters are not as I used to imagine: either you possess the world through money and power or you possess it through appropriation of values renouncing materialism. No, there are more possibilities and more motives, and they cannot be classified. There is also the question of using guile against the power of time. Can we possess it, can we control it? Is our problem always in relation to time? What makes us closer to its truth?

After we parted, I continued for a long while to think of "my time" through my experience with Ghaylana and through my experience with her daughter, Fatima. I felt I existed outside normal time. Illusions. Running after moments to renew the bygone past, the present is in the grip of attrition. There is no escape, I now realize that disintegration is coming; its steps are advancing and devastating, no illusion can stop them, no furtive enjoyment, no invention of wingèd forms or worlds.

I am as distant from Ghaylana as she is from her daughter, and they are both as distant from me as I am from the movement of these waves I see every morning from this veranda. Everything affirms the truism of this separation. How can I therefore continue to claim to myself that there is a horizon for our meeting and coming together again?

In the Evening

Stagnation and viscosity. Nameless monotony. My mind takes me to what Joséo related to me about the carnivals of international Tangier.

Before 1936 Tangier had an annual carnival lasting several days. It began on Thursday in the middle of Great Lent. There was a magnificent parade in which twenty folkloric carts participated, carrying beauty queens accompanied by groups of figures with huge heads having caricatural features painted in color on cardboard masks. Fantastic, comic faces. In the same parade, there were motorcars that were the first automobiles ever to reach Tangier from Europe; they were decked with flowers and colored ribbons, and they moved slowly as they received shouts of acclamation and admiration from the excited onlookers on both sides of the street. In those days, men were fond of straw hats similar to that of singer Maurice Chevalier. They wore them and entered the fray of throwing confetti, flower petals, and serpentine ribbons at one another. Merriment and joy continued for several days.

In those carnivals, platforms were erected for the representatives of the nine states and the notables to sit on. Carnations and jasmine were thrown from those platforms at the procession of beautiful women gleaming among the masked faces. The days of the carnival ended with a grand ball called "baile de pinata," held at the Cervantes Theater toward the end of the evening; the participants in it danced the tango, the samba, the Charleston, and the paso doble popular at that time . . .

As I recalled what Joséo related to me about the carnivals of international Tangier, I thought of carrying a placard throughout the city, with the following written in red on it: "I demand a carnival that will save Tangier from its official holidays and ceremonies."

In the Evening

I read what the Japanese painter Hokusai wrote about his relation to painting and I found in it some of what I myself feel:

Since I turned fifty, I have painted a number of tableaux. But among all my paintings before I became seventy, there is nothing of any great value. At seventy-three, I began to understand some of the real qualities of birds, animals, and insects and some aspects of the vital nature of plants and trees. Therefore at eighty, I will have achieved some progress; and at the age of one hundred, I will become a really wonderful painter. At one hundred and ten, every point and every line in my paintings will have a special life.

But Hokusai died at the age of eighty-nine and so he did not have the opportunity to reach the happy stage of excellence he had foreseen.

This is how the reality of painting, mixed with my own reality, appears to me: I always postpone announcing that I have got hold of it, because it is mercurial, multiple; and whenever I am close to it, it escapes. I may say the same thing about Tangier, whose multiple, changing faces are not loyal to any one of its conditions.

In the Morning

I read in the newspapers about the American millionaire Malcolm Forbes' celebrating his seventieth birthday in Tangier. He had bought the Commissioner's palace overlooking the sea. Does he now want to restore to Tangier some of its night revelry that it knew inside the palace of Barbara Hutton?

Forbes invited seven hundred of his friends and they will be flown in his own Boeing 727 named "Capitalist Tool." Among the guests are Elizabeth Taylor, Henry Kissinger, and "perhaps President Jimmy Carter whose presence has not yet been confirmed." During the ceremonies, Moroccan folkloric shows will be presented along with other musical and dancing shows to be presented by troupes coming from Europe and America.

Forbes announced that he will give each of his guests a copy of his new book, *More Than I Dreamt Of*, in which he tells the story of his life.

Two days later, I saw clips on television about Malcolm Forbes's ceremonies. I could hardly believe: splendid clothes, men and women like those we see in magnificent Hollywood films, piles of royal pink shrimps, glistening roasted lambs, gigantic cakes of strange shapes . . . The camera stopped at Elizabeth Taylor's round face and smiling eyes as though she were not past sixty . . . Then there was Moroccan folklore represented by songstresses, mountain and *ahwash* dances, and horsemen's gunshots . . .

Doubtlessly, Malcolm Forbes realized the meaning of happiness that night, despite his seventy years. No doubt, Tangier too was joyful to add that historic night to its former glories, a night etched in the memory of those attending and those who watched it on television or in the movies.

At the End of Night

I read:

"Real life means inventing new places so that we may not drown . . . And every new literary work is nothing but an invention of a new death."

In the Morning

I no longer feel enthusiastic about continuing to write these memoirs. Their idea came to me when Ghaylana left me and I found I was in a state of constant grief. I said I would resort to writing in order to understand what happened and still happens, after having lived my life responding to internal forces and physical impulses that could not be resisted. My paintings no longer suffice to weave veils that separate me from the world, from myself, and from my questions.

After her departure, many gaps were opened in my depths and around me. I failed to find refuge in indifference and the logic of strong things. I don't have any experience in writing and yet I began to gather certain aspects of my life or things related to my obsessive meditations. Contrary to painting, words seem to me "vulgar," direct abbreviations of what I have been feeling for some time in my depths.

I tore up many pages because I found their tone too sure and definitive, especially with regard to the experiences I lived . . . As I thought again of those experiences, without words, they appeared to me to be equivocal, contradictory, lacking the logic that words gave them. I thought to myself, "Let me go along with my thoughts as they come, without attention to sequence or linkage . . . Let the writing be in paragraphs that glow or fade, following the flow of my inner rhythm." I found that I dozed, I mean that I wrote a page or half a page, then resumed writing only after several months, during which I continued to turn around in my mind what I had written: Did it really have the fingerprints of my life? Is its language close to mine or is it an echo of it? Will others understand these fragments as part of a larger space of complex layers?

In painting, I found a sort of solution as expressed by one critic, namely, that the space of a tableau is necessarily a duplication of the self and a material separation of it from the world . . . Hence, the space of painting is pure, it is totally dreamt of.

But as I try writing, I do not find that words separate me fully from their extension to what surrounds me and what is stored in my memory. And although, when I started writing these memoirs, the matter had to do with recalling fragments of space that I crossed or that crossed me, I was soon overtaken by an ambition to specify that space in words so that it too may be dreamt of, separated from my memory and its lived experiences, duplicating my self and its manifestations, and thus making my memoirs give me the pleasure of being more than one face, one course, and one experience. I am not a social or political personality, and people of Tangier don't consider me as one of the "town's elite," and I don't intend to embellish my biography by these memoirs or polish my image . . . I was seeking understanding but I found myself pulled toward creating the pleasure of space covered by dreams and exuding illusions and hallucinations. .

What's gone is gone and you have space, of which to dream; everything else is prattle and sermonizing blown by the winds. Survey all the experiences you lived through or you imagined you lived through. Collect all the faces and specters of women and men who crossed your space, and look whether you have the power to represent them and move them again. There is no harm in recalling names: your mother, Ghaylana, Joséo, al-Zulali, al-Dahmani, Kanza, the barber of Marrakesh, Hadidesh, Fatima

. . . There is no harm either in remembering places:Tangier, Fez, Marrakesh, Spain . . . But in the midst of this disparate heap, how will you make yourself speak the language you spoke when you lived with them? Will you capture, as you write it, the freshness of feeling and expression? That may not be essential . . . More important is how you will fill the abyss that has separated you from the outside world since your attitudes and words secretly lost all credibility, and you have become an actor in a troupe with innumerable members, who play a role in a drama directed by a one-eyed fate or a blind will? Can you deny, as you pronounce your name, al-'Ayshuni, that a strange echo hits your eardrums, conveying the scum of your cracked identity, your smashed integrity, your vanished love?

All this is not important now, so long as enthusiasm has gone and I am no longer able to continue these memoirs. Returning to painting may perhaps be suitable to keep together many things that are not possible for me to separate from one another; whereas words necessarily require such separation and accuracy.

But what I wrote in these notebooks has become very dear to me, it has become part of "another person" dwelling deep in my depths. That's why I don't want to tear them up. Yesterday, I thought of giving a copy of them to one of my friends, a novelist by profession, to use them as the central plot of an exciting novel he will write. More than that, I will offer him probabilities that seem possible for composing my story with Ghaylana and Fatima, and what I reaped in about sixty years. I record here three probabilities, to which I will not hold him, for his imagination may open up to other probabilities:

1. A description of Tangier in the days of the international regime, using historical documents:
- Reconstitution of my family's way of life in Dwar Lakhrab, after the novelist visits my village.
- Details of how Joséo brought me up after adopting me.
- My adolescence and youth in the "wild years" and my relationship with Ghaylana.
- Ghaylana's marriage and her moving to Fez in the 1950s.
- Change in behavior and values after independence—Ghaylana's emigration to Spain.
- Her daughter Fatima's life in Fez, her experience at the university, and her story with al-Dawoodi.
- The social and political atmosphere of the 1970s.
- Fatima's emigration to France.

2. The novelist can make Fatima the point of departure when, after her trip to Paris, she decides to write a testimony entitled "Me, my mother, and her lover," in which she relates her experience in post-independence Morocco, using my memoirs to show the differences between a painter's nostalgic reflections and the harsh realities she and Ghaylana lived through.

3. The text begins with Fatima's visit to al-'Ayshuni at his home (that is myself, turned into a fictional character). She is motivated to visit him by her curiosity to get acquainted with her mother's sweetheart. She has an adventurous love affair with him, interspersed with dialogues and questions about her mother and his life. Then she departs without leaving an address. Ghaylana comes to visit al-'Ayshuni more than a year later, having been as-

sailed by the signs of old age, to complain to him bitterly about her daughter . . . Al-'Ayshuni later receives a letter from Fatima telling him about her life in Fez, her adventures in Paris, and her capture of a wealthy husband who saves her from vagrancy and selling her body. If the novelist chooses this format, he can use here paragraphs from my notebooks and he can as well cite fragments from them as he represents certain positions . . .

But there may be a fourth probability and a fifth one when these memoirs are turned into a novel.

My novelist friend is the one who will choose the form, the details, and the composition, if he agrees to write the novel.

There is an idea I want to suggest so that the novel's text may contain it, for I could not insert it within the reflections I recorded in these notebooks. It is an idea that continuously slips away from me, although it comes to my mind whenever I survey my life and my relationship with Ghaylana and Fatima. We have always existed on the margin, compared to those who consider themselves the "town's elite" and guardians of its traditions and conventions. When I look around me, I find many like us who multiply at a frightful rate . . . Will this not lead to a change so that those on the margin will besiege those in the center?

This is not the idea as I have felt it, strong and suggestive, before I put it in these words. I think that, when I advise my novelist friend to present this idea, he will respond by using the same answer the poet Mallarmé gave the painter Degas when the latter wrote a poem filled with many ideas: "It is not with ideas that a poem is written but with words." I have to return to lines and colors. I don't think it is unlikely that my novelist friend will laugh at me and say, "What's with you and words?" Then I will adopt the voice of one novelist and say to him, "I've written these words because of my weakness. If I were strong, I would have written nothing. If I were strong, I would have tamed life and become master of my desires and the desires of others."

I have therefore to return to lines and colors in order to follow the fugitive light that constantly escapes from me . . . It is a light that does not need words. It surprises me when I open my eyes on certain mornings and find it pouring from the sky of Tangier, transparent, sparkling, manifesting all differences and details in things so clearly that they appear to be transfigured. I wonder: How can I lodge this light on canvas, with all its density and invasiveness?

When I mix my colors and begin to paint, the luminosity surrounding me begins to be transferred to my canvas as a piercing brilliance, from whose flashes filters the hue of a light that is diffused as it embodies the contours of my dream's space. Running after the fugitive light is an act full of torment but it exudes pleasure and the enticements of mirage . . . It can never be compared to the sterile act of searching for words to capture shreds of stored feelings.

Who among us does not run away from something? I return to my lines and colors: I run away from the words of these memoirs and renounce the illusion of recording through them the experiences I lived. I am content to repeat: What's gone is gone. Light and color are what remain for me, and also space—of which I dream through them . . . Everything else is prattle and sermonizing blown by the winds.